I0684567

# "Deus Ex Machina"

## 'A Fractured Heroic Anthology'

by,

Robert A. Boyd

Consulting Redneck:

J. Rob O'neill

ISBN: 978-0-9851547-9-0
English Trade Paperback Edition

Proceeds from the sale of this work go to support self-published and small press authorship.  If you wish to aid this effort, please go to the publisher's website —

The-Written-Wyrd.org

—for further information.

Thank you.

§

*This is a work of fiction.  Any resemblance between the characters portrayed and actual persons, living or dead, is purely coincidental.*

\*\*\*\*\*

# Contents:

Readers are cautioned that the Author and Publisher cannot assume responsibility for apoplexy, hysterics, twisted world views, or Righteous Butt-Hurt resulting from reading this volume.

Enter at your own risk.   Just sayin'.

# "Ogre The Unspeakable"

It was a dark and stormy night in the Imperial trading village of Schadenfreude; much like any night in this dank, miserable outpost huddled in the middle of nowhere.  The wind howled like lost souls whom the Gods were exacting *personal* vengeance upon, and the driving rain roiled the muddy streets into torrents.  The villagers huddled by their fires, listened to their wretched hovels creaking, and prayed the Storm Giants would go pick on some *other* miserable, misbegotten village.  But the Gods have a thing for nights like this, bastards, so they cowered by their meager hearths, cursed their ill lot, and endured as best they could.

Despite that bummer opening, it was business as usual in the Last Man Standing inn: a despicable hole, the unofficial center of the Thieves', Degenerates', Sociopaths' And All-Round Losers' Quarter.  The place was packed with the usual fugitives, escaped slaves, wandering vagabonds, Black Mages, and other riff-raff, so, yeah, the party was *on* regardless of the weather.

The air was rank with stale urine, stale cooking, stale beer, and stale *tralla* smoke.  The crowd was stale too, with drunken good cheer.  Several of them were ravaging one of the serving wenches, while six more lay on the floor: one violently dead, one dying, one passed-out drunk, one stoned, one tearing at his clothes and screaming about spiders, and one having just been cold-cocked by a slaver's press gang.  The adjectives flew thick and fast that night, and the local authorities long since gave up trying to get a decent story out of this place; a typical night, as was said before.

Of all that earthy, villainous crew, the earthiest and villainousest sat at the table furthest from the door (the dubious honor in this dubious place).  The larger was known as Ogre: so-called since he bore an unhealthy resemblance to those *creatures*, and because he couldn't remember his real name.  Not much was known about Ogre, other than that he was a brutish troglodyte from the hill country who was sentenced to life in the salt mines (a short sentence, true) for ravaging an Imperial handmaiden.  He broke out of there, so legends say, killing twelve guards in the process, and took up the skittish life of a thief and reaver.  That seemed a bit far-fetched for his obvious limitations, but no one had the nerve to say so out loud.

Ogre seldom showed any emotion other than blood rage or utter confusion, but for now he was momentarily content...and a bit frustrated. The contentment was simple enough: while he lacked the wit to come in out of the rain, he at least understood there was no grog out in the street, so his thirst led him here a few hours earlier to a belly full of meat and his fifth or sixth tankard. His frustration...more on that in a moment.

The smaller fellow sitting next to him was Mouse, a typical thief. He was about as opposite to Ogre as one could be: short, slender, timid and quick-witted. He liked to think of himself (and was thought of by all who knew them) as Ogre's better half (out loud) or the brains of their duo (in private). In an odd way, thieves' status depends on their protector, and few indeed failed to show deference with Ogre looming in the background. While he often looked askance at Ogre's behavior, he nonetheless parlayed that deference into a cushy racket bringing him more loot and informal favors than Ogre knew about, or likely could comprehend.

They met two years ago during a particularly bloody escapade which netted a huge purse of gold and twelve more dead, followed by an epic bout of drinking and carousing which made Ogre the stuff of (lurid and vulgar) legends. Mouse thought at first that Ogre was a uniquely bold and successful heathen, but came to realize lately he was simply too stupid to know when to quit. Still, the money was good (he made a point of handling their finances), and if he spent a part of each day running for his life, at least it kept him fit.

Anyway: Ogre's frustration. The three things Ogre liked most in life were stealing, killing, drinking, and wenching—all right, four things. He had already slaked his lust for the first two by robbing an Imperial tax collector and killing twelve of the City Watch. He was now well into his cups, for the third item, and was vaguely wondering how he would satisfy his fourth. This was how his day usually went, and he would be hard put to change that ingrained pattern, but there was no outlet for item four in sight...hence the frustration.

He watched the group assaulting the serving wench for some time, which was starting to get under his skin, but the idea of getting someone to *stop* ravaging her so he could *start* was too much for his feeble imagination. The other tavern wench was hiding behind the bar (he at least understood assaulting the barkeep meant no more ale), and the only other woman there was a slave girl who clung nervously to a warrior almost as big as he was. Ogre watched him for some time, noting his great big muscles and his great big sword, and wondered about killing him (first item). But he was preoccupied with sex (fourth item) at the moment, and changing mental gears took way too much effort.

So his frustration simmered, building slowly as he slammed ale shots with ale chasers, and munched a ham bone. He watched the room quietly, like a wild animal, while Mouse watched him nervously and kept ready to dive for cover when the need arose.

It must have been midnight when the door opened, letting out a cloud of foul air and admitting a tall stranger dressed in full cape and hood. Few noticed at first aside from Ogre, who wondered vaguely if this was someone to rob first and then kill, or kill first and then rob. He was sinking into total confusion over that when the stranger threw the hood back, revealing a bold, aristocratic face with piercing blue eyes wreathed in shimmering red hair. It was a woman!

The room fell silent as she doffed her cape with one swift flourish, revealing her stunning figure. She was as tall as most men, with fulsome hips, long legs and a rampaging bosom barely contained by a straining chain mail bodice. Her fiery red hair fell in a shimmering cascade to her waist, framing her bare midriff, while her chain mail thong held a drinking cup, a leather purse, and precious little else.

The villainous mob made way for her in awe as she approached the bar. The look in her eyes commanded respect, her cleavage cleared the path like a battering ram. It was plain to all this was *not* someone to mess with. She paused to exchange looks with that great big warrior with the great big muscles and his great big sword: he faded cautiously into the background, leaving her his place at the bar.

"Woman," Ogre muttered, which showed how entranced he was to get big words like that right. His long-simmering frustration exploded in a flood tide of testosterone. "Me want!"

"Ogre, that's a Barbarian Warrior Babe!" Mouse hissed. "Steer clear of her!"

That confused him, which wasn't difficult. "Huh?"

"She's a real live Barbarian Warrior Babe! She can clean out any tavern in the Thieves', Degenerates', Sociopaths' And All-Round Losers' Quarter without half-trying!"

Ogre eyed her skeptically. "She not have sword."

"She doesn't *need* a sword, trust me!"

But he was drooling by that point, not that he ever listened anyway. "Ogre want!" He stood abruptly and shoved the table aside. Mouse managed a hasty catch of his mug, saving most of his ale, and protested feebly as Ogre advanced on her like a one-troglodyte conquering horde. He shoved two earthy villains aside —the rest scattered like wind-blown leaves—came up behind her and confronted her at the bar. "I'll have you, wench!"

She paused to give him a contemptuous once-over, then turned, put her hands on the bar, vaulted up on it, and sat facing him. "What did you say?" she asked with a cool look.

That also confused him, since his conquests usually fainted dead away or ran screaming at the sight of him. "Uh...I'll have you, wench!" he repeated.

"Will you now?"

But Ogre never was one for lengthy courtships, and he never met a female yet who could play hard-to-get with him for long. His courting skills exhausted, he tackled her, wrapping both arms around her waist intent on pulling her to the floor where matters would proceed in typical rugged Ogre fashion. Then she grabbed his hair and pulled his face against her chest right between her massive breasts. For a moment, Ogre thought his wildest fantasies of eager women were *at last* coming true, but then she twitched her shoulders—first the right, then the left—taking an exaggerated roundhouse swing with each. Her huge, solid breasts wrapped in hard, heavy chain mail smacked him up-side the head with a cringe-inducing *WHAP! WHAP!*, and he dropped in a heap.

"I warned him," Mouse muttered in the silence which followed. "Didn't I warn him?"

She sat on the bar and looked down at Ogre with a disdainful sneer as she swayed gently back and forth until the oscillations in her cleavage dampened out, then looked up at the stunned figures around her. "Next?"

Dead silence. Even the wind stopped howling.

She twitched her shoulders again, evoking a collective whimper from the mob as she shimmied lethally. Once she saw they were properly cowed, she slid off the bar, dug a pence out of her pouch, and slapped it down in front of the stunned barkeep. "A mug of ale, and not the cheap rotgut you usually serve!" she snapped. Then she paused to kick at Ogre, who lay moaning on the floor with a broken jaw, six teeth gone, and a concussion. "And get someone to clean this floor while you're at it."

\*\*\*\*\*

# "Do Not Metal In The Affairs Of Wizards"

"Honestly, Am-kashra, you're starting to worry me," Zin-eroth the Blue grumbled. "Your obsession with this non-mystical mumbo-jumbo is getting to be, well, an obsession. Whoever heard of a non-magical universe, anyway?"

"Hey, I'm entitled to a hobby on my days off." Normally Am-kashra the Green was a good-natured sort, but his interest in the legends of a universe with no magic in it earned him more than his share of grumbling from the locals. He could expect it from them, but it irked him that his friend and fellow professional didn't have a bit more faith in him. "Besides, I've made more progress then you might imagine."

"Uh-huh. And what will you tell the village elders if you succeed? They aren't thrilled with you as is."

Am-kashra looked askance at him. "That was just a phase, all right? I'm over that now, and most of the young ones turned out well enough."

"Statistically speaking. There were enough of them."

"Yeah, and one of them was the grandfather of the village headman; at least *he* should cut me some slack."

Am-kashra represented the Fertility Goddess, and his role in the village was performing growth and flowering magic to insure a bountiful harvest. It was a good living for a wizard. He enjoyed a steady income and plenty of free time in the winters, aside from blessing the calves and the new crop of infants, to pursue his hobbies.

And therein was the problem: Am-kashra was bored with the mediocre life of a village wizard. *All* the time with the fertility spells *and* the growth spells *and* the bounty spells, *day* in and *day* out with the *bumper* harvests and the *laden* vineyards and the *fecund* herds; it was enough to drive him to tears at times. Truth, he was in a rut. Serving the Fertility Goddess was a good career for a nibbish like him, but he longed for *adventure* in his life.

"The headman isn't exactly in a 'slacking' mood," Zin-eroth assured him. "And it doesn't help your cause that half the council are short and chubby and named after you."

Am-kashra paused digging through his pile of scrolls to give Zin-eroth a theatrical sigh. "*So* petty! Doesn't he have anything better to do?"

"Well there *is* the ongoing effort to clean up the village's ripe reputation."

"Picky, picky, picky! Didn't all the tourism help our economy? What does he want, anyway?"

His problems with the council started innocently enough: applying bounty spells to underdeveloped lasses. It wasn't long before temptation beckoned—he did represent the Fertility Goddess, after all—and he began taking the results for a test ride, with predictable consequences.

"It was the *sort* of tourists he objected to. Some people lose their perspective at the sight of all those bulging bodices."

"I swear I don't know what gets into *some* people. Bless the Goddess' fertility-obsessed heart; can't they just accept a simple act of piety?"

Chastised by the elders, he found himself back to square one: *all* the time with the fertility spells *and* the growth spells *and* the bounty spells, *day* in and *day* out with the *bumper* harvests and the *laden* vineyards and the *fecund* herds... Sigh.

So it wasn't long before his frustration embroiled him in a new hobby: experimental magic; the real out-there stuff on the cutting edge. And he was good at it, too, having dabbled for over two hundred years now. Lately he made a major breakthrough, so he claimed, and invited his friend, the village weather wizard, to see the result.

Zin-eroth came reluctantly since his *friend* had a history of more enthusiasm than common sense. Am-kashra's laboratory was a derelict warehouse on the outskirts of the village. He took it over many years ago, repaired the ramshackle eyesore, and converted it into his inner sanctum. It *seemed* like a happy working relationship between the villagers and their chastened Green wizard: they got some civic improvements and a little peace and quiet out of the deal, so what's not to love? (Little did they know what sort of experiments he was conducting in here; he'd learned.) Zin-eroth was expecting trouble.

"You don't really expect to achieve anything, do you?" He protested. "This stuff about a mundane universe is just a fairy tale! One for particularly stupid fairies, at that."

"Up yours, asshole!"

Zin-eroth turned angrily to find the heckler—and saw a glow of fairy-fyre strong enough to see in broad daylight coming from the next room. Am-kashra was preoccupied going through his magical artifacts, so Zin-eroth drifted over to see what was going on. His curiosity was rewarded by a bizarre sight. A wide area of the floor in the main room appeared to be solid gold, in the center of which stood a huge box. Around the box, at the edge of the gold area, a row of fairies fluttered along at waist height in a conga line flashing their fairy-fyre on and off like red strobes. They must have been under a Compulsion cast by Am-kashra and were in a foul temper about it. A couple of them made rude gestures at him.

Intrigued, Zin-eroth walked slowly around the huge box, eying it from all sides. It was taller than a man, roughly as wide, perhaps 20 paces long and made out of heavy corrugated panels. At one end was a pair of recessed doors held closed with massive vertical locking bars operated by handles set at a convenient height. It was painted a faded blue, badly weather worn, with various arcane markings on its ends and sides, the largest being:

# NIPPON CONTAINER LINE

"Fascinating!" Zin-eroth studied the mysterious insignia for a moment then tried to use his Insight to interpret it. No luck. His spell simply vanished into the blue-painted enigma. Frustrated, he pushed his way through the conga line of fairies who tried to hold him back with unwilling cries of "Stop! Danger! Go back!" and reached up to touch it...

"NO!" Am-kashra screamed from the doorway behind him. Zin-eroth jerked his hand away in confusion "That box is from the mundane universe!"

"It is?" Zin-eroth stepped back and examined it more cautiously. "This is really a mundane artifact? No magic in it at all?" He could see now why Am-kashra went to the trouble to cast a Compulsion spell on so many fairies to act as a warning line, which alone should have clued him to the importance—and the danger—of this artifact.

"That's right, and if you touch it, it'll suck the *mana* right out of you!"

Zin-eroth shivered in horror. This was something completely non-magical! Was it even possible? It seemed ordinary enough. One might almost mistake it for a storage shed of some slightly odd styling. But now he thought about it, Zin-eroth could feel the aching emptiness. This innocent-looking box was actually a non-magical void. Am-kashra had succeeded at something impossible—and horribly alien.

"So what is this thing, anyway?" he asked at last.

"Not being a complete fool," Am-kashra said archly, "I decided it was best to do a bit of ground work before trying anything ambitious." He made a sweeping gesture taking in the enormous box with a look of self-satisfaction. "Before I try to summon a mundane creature, I want to be sure I have some way to control it. Since any creature we summon from the mundane universe would not have any magic, we can't assume magic would affect it. So I arranged for this...container...to hold it."

"But...how?" Zin-eroth was at a loss. A cardinal rule of magic was that one must be familiar with the subject being summoned. "Nothing has ever been summoned from the mundane universe. Most wizards don't even believe it to exist! How did you manage this?"

Am-kashra smiled. "That's my secret success!" He turned to a nearby table with a small wooden box sitting on it. "It took several years of research, but I finally worked out a spell for summoning something based on a symbolic model of what I wanted. I specifically wanted a large, heavy box to contain a mundane creature, so I used this model as a sample, and that iron chamber is what I got." He rested his hand on the small model possessively.

"Brilliant!" Zin-eroth muttered. "Er...did you say *iron?*"

"Yes!" Am-kashra waved an arm at the huge construct. "The entire thing is solid iron, if you can believe it!"

"Incredible! But where could they find a meteor that large?"

"No, it's plain iron, like you dig out of the ground."

That was a sobering thought. Am-kashra was fooling with something only used by swordsmen. Now that he looked closely, Zin-eroth could see the rust stains where the paint was worn away.

"But who would build something this big out of solid iron?"

"No idea, but they must have formidable blacksmiths."

Iron is the best substance for carrying a magical spell, which is why swordsmen insist on using it to make weapons: they can be enchanted with all sorts of nasty striking and slicing and blocking spells. But an iron artifact much larger than a sword was unheard of. Moreover, this box shape would be a natural accumulator of spell power...but it came from a non-magical universe. The potential conflicts were entirely unpredictable. This was dangerous territory they were entering.

"What did they use it for if they have no magic?"

That stumped Am-kashra, and after a moment he answered softly, "I honestly don't know. There is so much we have yet to learn about the mundane universe. All I can tell you is it was filled with those." He gestured across the room to a low wall of boxes formed of thick paper, all identical, all inscribed with a large logo reading:

SONY
Playstation

"It took me three days to unload the container, and I stacked them there to get them out of the way. They're not very heavy, whatever's in them."

That brought up an obvious problem. "So how were you able to handle them if they are non-magical? And for that matter, why doesn't this...container...draw *mana* from the ground? I happen to know there are several centuries of crop and mercantile magic accumulated in this warehouse."

Am-kashra pointed at the floor. "I'm not nearly as stupid as I look! See for yourself!" The gold colored area proved, on close inspection, to be gold paint. There were also thin blocks of gold under each corner of the mundane container.

"Ah! I see!" Gold is magically neutral and will not carry a spell, which is what makes it so valuable. "But this must have cost you a fortune!"

"You have no idea." Am-kashra rolled his eyes comically. "And then there were these." He gestured to two sets of boot covers, heavy gloves and full length aprons made of cloth-of-gold hanging on the wall by the door.

"Protective gear," Zin-eroth grunted. "Well I'm glad to see you are taking *some* common sense precautions, anyway. Good thinking about the cloth-of-gold." He turned back to face his friend, "So what happens now? You said you would provide a demonstration?"

Am-kashra produced the scroll he was hunting in his work room. "Today I'll try to summon a creature from the mundane universe and have it arrive inside there."

Zin-eroth looked askance at him. "Oh, that's all? You'll just summon some...Gods know what from *somewhere* the Gods themselves likely don't know about, and have it *appear* in that box? You know how delicate summoning is. Do you have any *idea* of how many ways this could go wrong?"

"Hey, it's a non-magical creature from a non-magical universe arriving inside a non-magical iron box sitting on non-magic-conducting gold. What could go wrong, huh?"

"I guess we'll find out."

"I guess we will." Am-kashra seemed far too sure of himself, as was only to be expected. "This will be easier than the original summoning since I can use the container itself as a touchstone. We will simply summon a creature that relates to it; far easier than fishing blind."

Even that proved easier said than done. After making the usual preparations, Am-kashra positioned himself on one side of the container, spread the scroll out on the table beside him and, wand raised, began chanting the spell slowly and carefully. The spell was long—very long, it turned out—and Am-kashra droned on for some time following a convoluted trail of penciled-in additions and corrections. It needed a lot of refinement, and he paused more than once to trace some scribbled notation before continuing cautiously.

At long last, with his voice getting hoarse, he completed the recitation with a flourish, then dropped his wand on the table and massaged his aching shoulder.

"*That* was easy?"

"Yeah, compared to the box."

There was a moment of silence: then came a strange...sucking...sensation, as if the magic in the room was being drained into a vortex. The fairies gave a collective squeal of terror when a muffled *Whump!* came from inside the container. Then there was nothing.

"Well?" Zin-eroth whispered hoarsely.

Am-kashra nodded. "There's something in there, all right. The question is, what? I guess there's only one way to find out."

"I was afraid you'd say that."

They donned the protective cloth-of-gold garments reluctantly, then paused in front of the container's double doors.

"Ready?" Am-kashra croaked. His hands were sweaty and he was trembling as he held the first door latch with his thick gloves.

Zin-eroth nodded, struggled to adjust his heavy apron and nervously gripped his wand with both hands. "Right. Do it."

Am-kashra forced the first handle up and twisted it to one side, releasing the locking bar. They stood for a long moment, too nervous to go on, before he grabbed the other handle and heaved it up. The door released with a metallic grunt. They swung it open and there at the far end of the container stood the mundane.

It was humanoid, more or less, but no one could mistake it for anything but what it was. It was as short as Am-kashra, but scrawny: almost famished, its features shrunken and yellowish as if it had starved. It was wearing a suit of ragged dark green clothes, soft shoes and a cap, all of which were battered and faded, and it carried what looked like a complex spear—some sort of constructed device with a wicked looking knife or short sword attached to its end.

As they opened the door, the creature backed against the far wall of the container, facing them with its device—clearly some sort of weapon—held pointing toward them. It must have been terrified by what just happened.

"Whatever it is, it's small enough that we can handle it," Am-kashra said with some relief.

"For that matter, it's aligned to green," Zin-eroth said doubtfully. True, its clothing was an odd shade of dark yellowish green, but green nonetheless. "You should be able to magically influence it..."

"BANZAI!!!!" the creature shrieked and lunged at them.

Zin-eroth instinctively hit it with a stun spell before Am-kashra could react. The spell staggered it slightly, but it kept coming. Am-kashra got over his surprise, leveled his wand and fired off a repulsion spell in turn. It did little more than slow the creature enough that Zin-eroth was able to avoid being skewered. The mundane collided with him and the two battled fiercely in the doorway, the mundane kicking and punching and shrieking in some unknown language. Zin-eroth was far taller and heavier than the creature, but he was clearly getting the worst of it. The mundane was rapidly pounding him into submission, and looked about to kill him altogether.

Thinking fast finally, Am-kashra took a half step back, leveled his wand at the creature's face with both hands and roared a repulsion spell. The spell caught it right on its chin, knocking its head back. It went slack for a moment, Zin-eroth was able to push it back into the container, and they hastily retreated and slammed the door. Am-kashra was trying to set the locking bolt when the creature hit the door from inside, nearly knocking them back, but they managed to force the door shut again and set the bars. They then backed away from the container, shaken and dismayed, as it pounded on the inside.

"You've summoned a monster!" Zin-eroth gasped as he clutched his belly with one arm and wiped his bloody nose with the other. "I never thought it was possible to be hit so hard in so many places so fast!"

"Success!" Am-kashra stood shaking and breathing hard, completely at a loss. "Gods help us."

"I don't understand why our spells didn't work!" Zin-eroth complained as he probed his groin gingerly. "We hit it with enough force to stop a giant, but it bounced off!"

"No." Am-kashra struggled to catch his breath. "The spells were being absorbed by the container, remember? It's a mundane object...er...what's that?"

Zin-eroth opened his hand and saw he was holding a small round object: a button, obviously torn from the creature's clothes during the struggle. "It's a button." he said, lamely.

"We might be able to learn something from it!" Am-kashra's normally effervescent spirits recovered instantly. "Come on! I've got something we can try!"

He turned on his heel, pushed through the conga line of fairies so rapidly that two of them were knocked loose, and disappeared into his inner sanctum. Zin-eroth staggered after him, getting another barrage of obscene gestures and cat-calls from the fairies, (nasty little buggers) and caught up with Am-kashra just as he was emerging from a drawer in his desk.

"We'll see what the Orb Of Comprehension has to say!" he bubbled with the easy enthusiasm which replaced his earlier pessimism like the turning of a page.

Zin-eroth halted abruptly at the sight of the Orb—a smooth, hand-sized sphere of gleaming black with a white infinity sign embossed on its top. "What're you doing with Black Magic?" he demanded.

"Relax! I picked this up by some bartering. All it does is reveal the hidden truth of things." He set the button on the table next to the Orb, and readied his wand. "What is this button?" he demanded, then waved his wand over the two objects, muttering a spell in Black speech. Zin-eroth winced at the sound, thinking he really needed to have a heart-to-heart talk with his friend. Soon. Incantation done, Am-kashra picked up the Orb and looked at the answer revealed on its flat base:

THE SIGNS POINT TO YES

"Yep," Zin-eroth grunted. "Heck of a deal you got there."

"Uh, well, I need more practice with this spell, is all." Am-kashra replaced the Orb and tried again, straining his voice. Retrieving the Orb, he checked the answer:

## TRY AGAIN LATER

"Okay," Zin-eroth nodded. "That tells us a whole lot more."

"One more try." Am-kashra replaced the Orb, pulled back the sleeves of his robe, took a deep breath and bellowed the Black spell as loud as he could, eyes pinched shut and his wand shaking in both hands. The light dimmed, the room shook, and the fairies in the other room set up a chorus of alarmed squeals. Finished, Am-kashra took a deep breath to settle his nerves, then grabbed the Orb again:

## IT SEEMS LIKELY

"*What* seems likely?" Zin-eroth grumbled. That thing is useless..." BANG! A metallic explosion and another chorus of fairy shrieks came from the other room.

"Now what?" Am-kashra cried.

BANG! Accompanied by the sound of breaking glass. Button forgotten, the two of them raced back into the main room, fighting their way through a flood of fleeing fairies.

BANG! Something whizzed past them as they came through the door and blasted a chunk out of the wall. Am-kashra grabbed Zin-eroth's arm and pulled him down behind the low wall of the paper boxes.

"You said it was mundane!" Zin-eroth gasped, the wind knocked out of him again. "It's hurling spells at us!"

"We'll see about that!" Am-kashra grunted. He jumped to his feet, waved his wand before them and yelled a spell of protection. A wall of immaterial power appeared between them and the container. "That's better!"

BANG! There were already several round holes punched in the side of the metal container, and now another appeared abruptly. "Ow!" Zin-eroth howled. Am-kashra turned and saw his friend had been grazed across his arm by another spell...

"Oh, crap!" he gasped, "It's not using magic!"

"It...WHAT?" Zin-eroth yelled in alarm as he tried to stem the blood soaking into his sleeve.

"It's from mundania!"  Am-kashra ducked behind the paper boxes again, "No magic!"  BANG! and something went right through the stacked boxes with a shattering glass sound, passed between them and buried itself in the wall.  "It's using some sort of weapon!"

"You mean you've got a *swordsman* in there?!"

"Um..."  It occurred to them, belatedly, that in a world with no magic, all they'd have is swordsmen.  "...it must have some sort of projectile launcher, like a crossbow..."

BANG!  Another chunk of the wall went flying and the two of them dove for cover again.  BANG!  One of the paper boxes split, showering them with bits of paper and glass and some unidentifiable material.

"That's no crossbow!"

Suddenly the banging was replaced by the sound of something heavy pounding on metal.  The two rolled to their knees and peered anxiously over the top of the paper boxes.  The side of the mundane container was riddled with holes in a close-set semicircle.  In one part of the circle, the iron had given away and now the mundane was pounding on the inside with his weapon.  As they watched, two sets of fingers appeared and the iron was bent back, leaving a small opening.

"It's escaping!" Zin-eroth gasped.  "Quick!  Do something!"

Then the mundane peered out through the opening, which was large enough to reveal part of its face.  Stupefied, the two wizards peered back and their eyes met for an instant.  What they saw shook them: this thing was a killer, and it wanted them, badly.  The mundane's face disappeared, and a hand reached through the opening and tossed a small object which landed opposite them.  The two wizards studied it in confusion.  It was round...gray...knobby...smoking...  Zin-eroth grabbed Am-kashra's arm and yanked him back down behind the boxes just as it exploded.  The room shook from the blast and the wall of paper cartons tumbled down on them.

"*What was that?*" Am-kashra gasped as he mopped his face.  He was bleeding from a scalp wound from a flying bit of metal.  It stung like crazy.

"That thing's going to kill us!" Zin-eroth pleaded with him. "We have to do something before it breaks out of there!"

Am-kashra was stunned from the force of the blast and partly blinded by blood and dust in his eyes. "...unh...you're right...any ideas?"

"What...um...uh...I don't know!" Zin-eroth gasped. "This is your spell!" BANG! The creature went back to punching holes in the container. "M-magic won't help! How about an Inverted Summoning?!"

"But that's an act of desperation! They told us in Wizard's Apprenticeship never to try it unless we're in big trouble."

"Trust me! We're in *big* trouble! Call that thing's counterpart to deal with it!"

"B-but there's no way of knowing what will appear. It might be destroyed itself. And whichever won, we'll have to deal with the survivor."

BANG! Am-kashra ducked as another projectile flew over their heads. "We don't have a choice! Do something fast before it breaks loose."

Am-kashra thought fast. "We'll have to combine the Inverted Summoning spell with my Symbolic Summoning spell. Get any part of it wrong and there was no telling what would happen!"

BANG! They both threw themselves flat as they were showered with plaster again.

"Well we know what'll happen if you do nothing!"

Am-kashra sighed. "I'll never hear the end of this."

Mind made up, he jumped to his feet, snatched the scroll where it lay on the table and dove back behind the wall of boxes. BANG! and another chunk of plaster flew as he feverishly began the incantation. It took several minutes of carefully muttered phrases, accompanied by whispered suggestions from Zin-eroth and several more BANGs! before they felt the bizarre sucking vortex sensation again.

BANG! Another hole appeared in the iron container...then...

They heard the muted *Whump!* of the summoning...then...

There was a moment's silence...then...

BANG! followed by a muffled exclamation...then...

20

BRRAAAPPPPPPP!!!! and the side of the iron container exploded outward under a shower of projectiles which chewed the wall of the warehouse and sent splinters flying in all directions. The two wizards scuttled the other way in panic, winding up cowering in the far corner at the end of the row of paper boxes. There was a long silence, except for the ringing in their ears from the multiple explosions and the occasional crunch of falling plaster. "You did it!" Zin-eroth hissed. "You summoned an even more powerful foe to defeat it!"

"Wonderful. Now what do we do?"

BRRAAAPPPPPPP!!!! Before they could come up with an idea, the partly completed semicircle of holes in the side of the container was extended by another shower of projectiles, which also tore up the heap of paper boxes where they huddled only moments before.

"Gods!" Zin-eroth gasped. "This one's escaping too!"

BRRAAAPPPPPPP!!!! Where the earlier mundane's weapon was potent, this one was ripping the heavy metal container to shreds. A second line of holes stitched the side, and the panel sagged. After a few seconds, there came a series of heavy thuds as the creature inside kicked the weakened panel. The torn metal buckled and fell away, leaving a man-sized hole, and the new mundane emerged.

"We're in it now," Zin-eroth mumbled.

This creature was larger than the other: almost as large as Zin-eroth, but lean, muscular and ragged. It was dressed in green clothing and heavy boots, wore a metal helmet and was carrying an even larger weapon than the first. Clearly this being was far more powerful than the other, who now lay crumpled against the inside wall of the container in a splatter of blood. The new mundane was covered with blood as well, showered all over it by its fallen foe and from a wound in its shoulder.

"They're both green," Zin-eroth whispered. "Why would two creatures aligned to green be enemies?"

"How am I supposed to understand non-magical thinking? It must be a mundane thing."

"You could have thought of that before you did this."

The creature's weapon was different too: with a leather shoulder strap to support its weight and a pair of stubby legs on the end, probably to stabilize it. Its front end was smoking, and from somewhere in its middle, a flexible strip of shiny brass cylinders emerged, draped around the mundane's neck and sagged almost to the floor.

"I only hope we can control this one now!" Zin-eroth hissed.

"We should be able to." Am-kashra watched it carefully between two paper cartons. "It's the natural enemy of the first one, which suggests it might not have any reason to harm us. And it is green, so I should be able to influence it." A muddy, dirty, bedraggled green, to be sure, but green nonetheless. He stood up carefully and addressed the mundane.

"Hello..."

The creature spun toward them. It was gasping for breath, its eyes wild with shock and rage, its limbs trembling with adrenalin.

"Thank you for slaying that creature. We're sorry to drag you here, but we..."

"SEMPER FI, SUMBITCH!!!!" it shrieked, and raised its weapon.

*****

# "Sir Hubris And The Dragon"

*Most people don't realize it, but dragons are not so much predators as scavengers. When one gets to be that large, pursuing a terrified animal through the forests is both energy-inefficient and hazardous to the wings. It's easier to steal the kills of lesser predators. That fundamental weakness has long been exploited by the Dragon Slayer's Order—so the Legends tell us...*

§

"Now try to remember what you've learned, if you can," yelled the Arms Master. "Saints know how you'll manage, may they have a sense of humor!"

Sir Hubris looked down at him from the back of his Hero horse, Testosterone, a view rather like looking out a second story window. Despite this unaccustomed perspective, he was eager to please his mentor, and followed every word with vast, laborious concentration. The pundits of a later age would mutter darkly about Pavlovian responses at the sight.

"This is important!" went on the Arms Master. "That beast is wreaking hell throughout the Kingdom! The King's Seneschal is raising an awful stink!"

In response to which, the Elders of the Order hemmed and hawed and pled various other duties. R H I P, then as always, and the task soon trickled down onto their newest member. So, filled with bubbling enthusiasm and not a little trepidation, Sir Hubris—bonged just that week—was about to go forth for the glory of the cause.

"Don't you worry, sir! I'm ready!" he assured the Arms Master. "I'll be all right!"

"The one thing I'm not worried about is *you*, you young whelp!" The Arms Master spat at his feet. "All that matters is that you uphold the honor of the Order!"

"I will sir! And I'll bring home that dragon's head! You'll be proud of me!"

"What*ever!*"

§

"Lor' bless ye, sir knight!" The villagers showed as much enthusiasm as they ever did as he set out from the Dragon Slayers' School. Dim-witted brutes, the lot of them, and he was thankful he'd escaped that life when he qualified for the Order. He was typical, this Sir Hubris, of the young knights of the Order: his decided lack of intellect being made up in sheer brawn. Raised on a lifelong regimen of red meat and day-long workouts, his thews rippled, and his bulging shoulders tapered without a neck into his sloping forehead. A Dragon Slayer, no doubt about it. To merely describe him as buff was disingenuous.

Buff, yes. Smart...well... His first check came a mere hundred paces from the School's gate, where the road went in two directions. It took him some time and carefully studying his instructions to find the correct way, and off he gallumped in search of adventure...

§

After four of his prized cattle vanished, the local Lord greeted him with more than the customary enthusiasm. "What do I pay my taxes for? Do something! That monster will begger me!"

He addressed Sir Hubris from the second story balcony of his manor house, which put him eye-to-eye with our Man-On-Horseback. Rubbing shoulders with commoners was contraindicated, then as always, and that lack of the common touch kept him from noticing his starveling peasants seemed a bit less starveling than usual. So the only logical explanation for the missing cattle (helped on by a few well-timed comments from the rank and file) was the culprit must be a dragon. QED. His frantic appeals to the Crown produced...this.

"And can't you do something about that...that...horse?" The combined weight of Sir Hubris and equipage kept pressing Testosterone's massive hooves into the ground, leaving the road in terrible shape. "Who's going to fill all those potholes?" The nearby peasants looked on glumly, knowing full well who would be filling all those potholes.

Like Sir Hubris, his Hero horse, Testosterone, was bred for the task, although one would wonder what breed he was. Slaying dragons takes enormous weapons; weapons which need huge

Heroes to handle them; Heroes who need lots and lots of armor to cover them; armor, weapons, saddle and rider in turn requiring a huge mount to move the whole shebang. All of which is to say Testosterone's ancestral Clydesdales would appear puny alongside him. He was also as dumb as rocks, the other breeding characteristic, since most horses won't charge a carnivore fifty times their size. He and Sir Hubris were a natural pair.

"Well? Are you just going to stand there blocking traffic? There's a monster out there!"

"Don't you worry, my lord! I am Sir Hubris, knight of the Dragon Slayers and devoted to your cause. I'll take care of that dragon for you!"

"What*ever.*"

§

Sir Hubris soon discovered that it's one thing to sit through lectures at the Order, another entirely to be out here in the wild looking for a carnivorous monster which could swallow him at a gulp. As he rode through the forest, he was starting to get the idea that this was not the brightest thing he'd ever done in his not very bright lifetime.

He had shadowed a pack of wolves for four days now, waiting for them to make a kill which would entice a dragon to him. Naturally the wolves resented his intrusion, but after Testosterone stepped on one of them, they figured anyone who would loiter around a pack of hungry wolves was too dangerous to tangle with. So everyone got along thereafter with only the occasional stand-offish snarl of disapproval.

At any rate, Sir Hubris found himself for the first time in his life with nothing to do but sit and think. He wasn't used to that, nor very good at it, and his mind was a turmoil of doubt. Dragons were so *freakin'* huge! It amazed him that anyone could kill one— as the knights of the Order did routinely, so they drilled into him. Truth, he had never seen a dragon, but the descriptions and drawings were graphic. *They* said it could be done; *they* showed him diagrams; *they* made him practice on the mockups again and again for *years*. Still, the whys and wherefores, and especially the *hows* were all he could fathom on good days. And there were

Questions he never considered before, like why were there dragons? Why did they have to be slain? And were a few cattle *really* such a large price to pay for peaceful coexistence? He was working himself into a dither trying to unscrew the inscrutable.

No matter; time to focus on issues at hand, which were taxing enough. The wolves finally brought down a moose, and were now greedily tearing at the carcass. The dragon he was after was somewhere down wind—off to the west, according to local rumors —and the smell of a fresh kill would soon draw it here. He chose his spot with care behind a huge oak tree on the upwind edge of the clearing where the wolves made their kill. Thus far, everything was going as he was taught, although more by luck than any design of his. Everything as ready as could be, he rested in his enormous contoured saddle to await events and tried to recall the details he'd learned at the school.

> *"The monster will come flying up wind to the scent of the kill and land with its back to you, which is the only way you'll last long enough to take a swipe at it. That's when you make your move, and Saints watch over you so you don't trip over your own feet!"*
>
> *"From behind, sir? Wouldn't it be more honorable to face it man to beast?"*
>
> *"If it wasn't a waste of a good suit of armor, I'd say go ahead and face the monster and be damned! Maybe it'll choke on you! I have often enough!"*
>
> *"But attacking from behind seems so...unheroic...sir!"*
>
> *"Heroism be damned! Charging a dragon face-on will get you toasted before you go twenty yards! The only way is to ambush the fiend! Down and give me fifty!"*

Honestly, in his early days, Sir Hubris wondered if his Arms Master knew what he was talking about. Presumably he did; he woke up screaming often enough. His hair had turned from bright red to pure snowy white by his time in the field, and he still drank far too much to control his shakes. But that and the loss of his arm did not keep him from limping around the training ground barking instructions and handing out pushups with ruthless fury, hammering the young acolytes into shape for the challenges ahead.

It happened this was the same region where his Arms Master forged his own legendary reputation, and Sir Hubris was dimly pleased to find *his* dragon in these same woods. What better place for a worshipful young knight to begin his career than in the footsteps of his mentor! He sighed as he recounted the heroic sagas of Dragon Slayer daring-do, of epic carnage and battle, of desperate feats of arms, of courage and suffering and grim endurance; forgetting for the moment that he was about to try the same damn-fool stunt himself.

§

The dragon appeared without warning, coasting in along the line of the valley and settling in the clearing with a billowing windstorm off its wings and an earthshaking *CRASH!* The wolf pack took one startled look and ran howling in terror as the dragon sent a spout of smoke and flame and a loud "Harumph!" after them...not so much a roar as a snort of derision. It then settled gracefully on its haunches and folded its vast wings with care, ready to enjoy a light snack of a ton of moose meat.

Hidden in the undergrowth, Sir Hubris sized up the monster. This was a Scottish dragon, according to his recognition chart, the give-away being its scales patterned in a brightly colored plaid (the Steward Tartan, in fact, not that Sir Hubris would recognize it). This was a male, and huge even by dragon standards, another spotting feature. He was also humming *'Scots Wha Hae'* in a melodious basso-profundo, which is a pretty obvious clue if all else fails. This old bull would make a grand trophy for a novice Hero!

This was the moment of truth. All of a sudden Sir Hubris' palms were sweaty and his mouth was dry. His Arms Master's exhortations echoing in his ears as he tightened his seat belt, dug his hips into the saddle and gave his shoulder harnesses one last anxious tug. Then, as ready as he would ever be, he reached for his dragon-slaying lance. The lance was solid forged iron, 40 feet long and so heavy it took six ordinary men to lift it. It was balanced just ahead of its grip on a swivel mount built into the massive saddle, with the shaft resting on the top of Testosterone's head. Sir Hubris leaned on the butt of the lance and the tip came up and centered on the dragon. Relieved of two hundred-odd pounds of dead weight, Testosterone's head hardly moved at all.

Steadying the heavy lance under his right shoulder, Sir Hubris then reached down with his left hand for the goad—a choke cable running down to the one spot where a prompt response could be expected, and the only way to get a Hero horse to charge.

The dragon was busy eating: it was now or never. Sir Hubris' breathing was quick and shallow, his heart racing, his Arms Master's echoed exhortations had become screams again. Stifling the instinct to cut and run, he took a deep breath and hauled on the goad for all he was worth.

Testosterone shuddered, emitted a shrill whinny and convulsed forth...ran SMACK! head-first into the oak tree, nearly tossing Sir Hubris...staggered a few steps to one side and charged again, this time more or less lined up on their target. THIS was the moment Sir Hubris lived for! Fear forgotten, he hauled feverishly on the goad as Testosterone responded with a series of agonized grunts and ever-greater efforts until they were pounding flat-out, ground shaking, clods of earth flying, Sir Hubris' shoulders rippling as he fought the wildly gyrating lance, struggling to hold it steady as they careened toward their prey!

§

Dragons are flying creatures, and their nervous systems have evolved to keep them in aeronautical trim at all times. So when the dragon heard the thunder of Testosterone's hooves, he lifted his head to see what was going on...and his tail automatically came up to counterbalance. The thundering noise was behind him, so he swung his head to the right...the upraised tail swung to the left...crossed the line of Sir Hubris' oncoming lance and...

## WHAM!!!

...the dragon was shoved forward about five feet, which simply doesn't happen to a top carnivore the size of a prosperous inn. Then came a cacophony of crashing, clattering, crunching, thudding and general collision-sounding noises from somewhere behind him. Continuing his head-turn, he found himself confronted by a sight which, frankly, left him speechless.

The end of his tail was run through by an enormous forged iron lance, four feet of the tip protruding beyond the point of impact. At the other end, now dangling some twenty feet above the ground, was the limp form of a large, muscular man dressed in battered plate armor and seated in an enormous high-backed saddle. He was connected to the butt of the lance by a couple of surviving leather straps and to the saddle by his seat belt and by his one serviceable arm, with which he was feebly trying to dig the saddle horn out of his groin.

Below this apparition lay the carcass of an enormous Hero horse in full armor, its narrow head shoved up the dragon's posterior to the shoulders. The impact tore the massive saddle girth loose, snapping the unfortunate Testosterone nearly in two.

Now...you must understand dragons are the smartest beings in the world, a lot smarter than Sir Hubris, certainly (which isn't saying much), but this inexplicable turn of events left him bewildered. More or less by reflex, he continued his head turn until he was looking back down his spine at Sir Hubris, who— because the dragon's tail mirrored the head movement—was rotated around until they met somewhere over the dragon's upper colon. They stared at each other for a bit, the dragon blinking his enormous eyes in confusion and Sir Hubris struggling to hold on to consciousness, they being nose to nose, as it were.

Then Sir Hubris watched in stunned dismay as the enormous mouth full of enormous teeth slowly gaped wide. He hung there paralyzed like a rabbit at the sight of that vast gullet stretching away down...down...down into the monster's innards. Poised above the ultimate gulp, he realized to his dismay that he was a failure as a Hero and, moreover, was about to become an appetizer for a ton of moose meat...

Then the nerve impulses arrived from the dragon's hindquarters (it was along trip) reminding him that Testosterone, now thrashing out one feeble last gasp, was wearing full articulated plate armor on the head, neck and shoulders lodged up his behind. There were spikes on that armor; it gave the dragon a burning, itching, all-round loose-in-the-caboose feeling. Most uncomfortable.

Said dragon paused and, rising to his haunches, gave a mighty grunting squeeze. There was a thunderous flatulent sound which echoed off the nearby hills, then the crashing, clattering, crunching, thudding and general collision-sounding noises again. Sir Hubris —still dangling at the end of his lance and hence from the end of the dragon's tail—was set swinging wildly by the gyrations. Before he passed out, he caught a momentary glimpse of Testosterone's body wrapped around the oak tree where they emerged from cover at the start of their charge.

§

There are some days when it just doesn't pay to regain consciousness, and this was shaping up to be one of them. Sir Hubris awoke thinking he must have had a particularly convoluted nightmare, but then the unsteady swaying and the pain in his everywhere told him this was no nightmare. No, this was much, much worse. Hesitantly, he opened one eye, hoping against all reason the dragon was merely a hallucination and he was safe in his bed back at the School. No School, no bed, and the dragon was still there. Damn.

Sir Hubris struggled to raise his head, and the two of them stared at each other as he pondered the situation. He was dangling in mid-air from the butt of his lance, nose-to-nose with an old bull Scottish dragon. (A Steward, at that.) His sword arm was useless, Testosterone was out of it, and even the wolves had deserted him. Yep. *'I'm dead'* summed it up nicely.

Then once again the enormous mouth full of enormous teeth slowly gaped wide. He hung paralyzed at the sight of that vast gullet stretching away down...down...down into the monster's innards in a really bad case of *déja vu* as he prayed for a swift death...

"That," quoth the dragon, "was r-r-r-rude!"

It took Sir Hubris a few seconds to realize the dragon was talking to him. Dragons can talk? They never told him about this in Dragon Slayer School! "Um..." offered he, confused.

"What d'ye think ye're doing, laddie?"

"Huh?" They didn't cover *this* in Dragon Slayer School either! But explanations were in order, so he better get to work and improvise. "Uh...well, you see...I was trying...um..." How does one put this delicately in such a situation? "I was...uh, well, I was trying to kill you," blurted out he at last.

*'Criminey!'* The dragon's reaction was plain in his weary expression. He emitted a deep sigh, and Sir Hubris squealed as an errant puff of flame singed his feet, convinced the monster was about to bar-b-que him.

"This is too much!" complained the dragon. "Canna a chap dine in peace? T'is ma first meal in a couple o' weeks, and ye've put me quite off ma feed."

"Um...sorry," gasped Sir Hubris. "It's nothing personal."

"An' look what ye did to ma tail!"

The dragon spun his tail around to examine the lance injury, sending Sir Hubris swinging in a wild arc. Fortunately he was at the far end of that swing when airsickness overtook him, so he missed the dragon again. Examination completed, the dragon snapped his tail back, sending Sir Hubris through a loop-de-loop in his saddle around the butt of the lance.

"That's going t' leave a scar!"

"P-p-please...d-don't...s-stop..." b-b-begged Sir Hubris as he struggled not to vomit again on the multiple dragon images floating around him.

"At least ye could say you're sorry!" The dragon gave his tail a flick, sending Sir Hubris through a couple more loop-de-loops.

"I-I-I-s-s-o-rrr-rrr-rrr-eee-eee!" croaked he, and let fly all over the dragon's left wing. The dragon surveyed the mess gloomily while Sir Hubris hung limp and gasped for breath. Whatever tiny chance he might have had just went bye-bye, but at least he felt a bit better.

"Kill me, ye say?" The dragon looked him over suspiciously.

"Umphhh, yeah..." Right then, all Sir Hubris wanted was for the dragon to eat him and have done with it.

"Now why would ye want t' do a thing like that?"

That was going to take more explaining than Sir Hubris was capable of at the moment. "Um..." repeated he.

"It's a machismo thing, isn't it?" The dragon pondered him for a bit, then settled comfortably on his haunches. "Look, laddie...this whole shining-armor thing can be ver-r-y seductive, ah understand that. And ah'm not faulting ye in the least, but ye've let it all go t'your wee head. Ah have t' admire your pluck, if not your sense of discretion, but ye need t' step back and get a new perspective on it all."

"Urppp..." Fortunately, nothing came up that time.

"Ah mean, we all have our inner demons," went on the dragon, earnestly. "And ah realize you're just trying t'cope with societal pressures, but ye've gotten into a negative reinforcement cycle. Ye really need to get a grip an' start defining your own space, instead of letting people manipulate ye like this."

Sir Hubris was usually confused by reasonable statements. "Wha d'ya mean?" gasped he.

"Don't ye see how this all ties into your childhood insecurities? Ye need to focus your youthful frustrations into some useful purpose. This destructive acting-out is only going to get ye in trouble some fine day."

That sort of talk made Sir Hubris feel very uncomfortable. "What would you know about my childhood?" angsted he. "You're the menace to society! You kill livestock!"

"Well, so do ye. That's what they're for." The dragon was trying to be reasonable, although it seemed like a futile effort. "And who was running around wi' that enormous toad sticker a minute ago? Maybe ye humans ought to focus t'killing each other off, hmmm?"

"A man has to do what a man has to do!" said Sir Hubris, with wounded dignity. Now the dragon's tail stopped whipping around, he was recovering somewhat.

"Whatever."

"And I do, too, serve a useful purpose! We protect the kingdom from monsters like you! Horrid, brutal, ravening..." the dragon raised an eyebrow, a disturbing sight "...uh...big, powerful...er...dragons..."

"An' ye expect me t'believe a puny wee laddie like you can kill one o' us?" The dragon seemed amused.

"Now you've gone too far!" huffed Sir Hubris. "I am a knight of the ancient and noble Order of the Dragon Slayers! Slaying dragons is what we do! Of course I could kill you!"

"*That* lot, eh? Ah should ha' guessed." The dragon sighed in exasperation. "An' just how many dragons d'ye suppose this Dragon Slayers' Order of yours has slain, hmmm?"

"Hundreds!"

The dragon raised another eyebrow.

"Ah...dozens, certainly!"

An amused grin, not a pretty sight.

"Um...How many?"

"Well, none *I've* heard of," replied the dragon with arch dignity. "Oh, there ha' been a few injuries...ouch! (the nerve impulse from the lance wound in his tail had just arrived)...but you're simply not in our league."

"Wrong, oh ungodly one! My hand is strengthened by our great motto, *'Stultus hero*...um...*heroica ineptias est considerare, et implere!'*"

"What?" The dragon smiled in amusement, another discomforting sight. "Find an idiot an' fill him full o' heroic nonsense? What sort o' motto is that?"

"You dare!" yelled Sir Hubris, in outrage.

"That's what ye said, in Latin. It figures, now ah consider it."

"Your crooked words cannot hide your fear!"

"Bad Latin, too. The syntax is all wrong."

"If you ever met one of us, you'd know your peril!"

"Eh? Well, actually, now ye mention it, ah did meet one of ye, about twenty years back." The dragon chuckled at the thought, not a pretty sound. "He wasn't much."

"Huh? Twenty years ago? You're sure?"

"Aye."

"In this area?"

"Aye."

"Red hair?"

"Um, aye."

"You bit his left arm off at the elbow?"

"Ah did that. Gristly it was, too, an' the horse he rode in on."

Sir Hubris sagged in dismay. His Arms Master! His spiritual mentor, his trainer, his whole life for as long as he could remember, a fake?

"But...but...that's impossible!" wailed he in anguish. "The Arms Master is a great warrior! He taught me everything I know!"

"Ye still don't get it, do ye laddie?" (The dragon put two and two together some time ago.) "They filled your wee head full o' heroic nonsense an' sent ye out here t' die just t' preserve their own tawdry sense o' self-importance."

That struck Sir Hubris dumb. The idea was ludicrous! The Dragon Slayers' Order was ancient and revered! Legends were told of their Heroes' might and courage! Bards sang the praises of the Dragon Slayers up and down the land! And now this...this...this...dragon!...had the nerve to claim it was all for nothing?

"What? We've never killed a dragon? That's silly! How do the Elders get the King to keep funding the Order?"

"Saints preserve ye, laddie, if ye canna figure that one."

That struck Sir Hubris even dumber. He brooded on it for a bit, then, "Um...I canna figure that one. Sorry."

"Look laddie, ah can see this is a big disappointment to ye. But life goes on. Ye're young an' healthy an' have a lot o' potential. Ah'm sure, with your martial training, ye can pick up a fine, steady job in law enforcement—a manly task, that—and ye can serve your community as well."

"Never!" Sir Hubris was appalled. "I'll never become a mere city Guardsman!

"An' I'll wager ye cut quite a swath wi' the ladies wi' your brawny build. Aye, that'll be the ticket! A steady job an' a fine plump lassie t' warm yer bed o' nights! That'll pick ye up an' set ye t' rights, forby!"

"But...I don't know any fine, plump lassies."

"Details, laddie! Details! Dinna fash yerself o'r it. D'ye quote any Byron, perchance?"

"Huh? Um, no, I don't." It never occurred to him to study Byron, not a tall priority back at the School. Who was Byron?

"Here's a passage ye might try:"

*"All my faults perchance thou knowest,"*
*"All my madness none can know,"*
*"All my hopes, where'er thou goest,"*
*"Wither, yet with thee they..."*

"Stop it! You're confusing me!"

"Laddie," grumbled the dragon, eyeing him severely, "ah'm tryin' t'help ye here. Ye could show a little appreciation o' the thought!"

"Help me? You're making my head hurt, you monster!"

"Well that's not surprising, seeing as ye only use it t' batter doors open wi!"

"I do not!"

"Well ye certainly don't use it for anything else or ye'd be more civil wi' someone who's looking t' help ye!"

"Help me? Help me, is it? What can you do for me, and who asked you anyway?"

"Ah'm tryin' t' help ye find some new line o' work, s'truth! Can ye not understand what we've been talking, or has the sun on that tin hat baked your wee brains?"

"Treacherous cur!" Sir Hubris kicked at the dragon in futile rage, setting his saddle rocking back and forth in mid-air. "I am a knight of the noble Order of the Dragon Slayers! I will never turn aside from the path of honor! *Stultus heroica*...um...*ineptias*..." he yelled, trying to draw his sword with his good arm.

"Oh, for cryin' out loud!" grumbled the dragon. "Ah dinna understand why ah put up with ye! Ah try t' help ye, but some people just won't listen!"

Rising to all fours, he gave a quick flick of his tail. The lance snapped, and Sir Hubris, saddle, lance butt and all, went sailing through the air to land in a stand of willow trees.

§

Regaining consciousness was a bad habit he really needed to break, he decided later. Speaking of which, it seemed the stand of willows broke his fall before he broke his neck. He hung upside down in the trees trying for some time to untangle himself from his saddle before he realized the dragon was still there, watching him.

"Laddie," grumbled he, "Ye really need t' work on yer people skills, forby!"

"Um...you're not going to eat me?"

"An' break a tooth on that thick skull o' yours?  Ah'm back t' Scotland where ah can dine in peace!"

§

Hanging there all alone gave him time to reflect (or maybe it was the blood rushing to his head) and at first he was appalled at his failure.  All his young life he dedicated himself to the Dragon Slayers' Order, and the result was so...so...humiliating!  He shuddered to think of what his Arms Master would say!

But after a while, the novelty of a talking dragon began to get under his skin.  And soon he began wondering about what the dragon said, about the Order and all.  Could there be anything to what he claimed?  The dragon never lied to him, certainly, and he seemed like a decent chap as Scottish dragons go.  And come to think of it, the Elders never did prove their claims.  But if that were so, then the Order was merely a self-perpetuating myth of glory, feeding on the blood of innocents to sustain their positions and their patronages and their exalted titles.  So who to believe?

It came down to the word of a dragon he had never been introduced to plus his own—albeit limited—experience in the art, against the character of his Arms Master and the Elders.

"It was all a friggin' lie!" moaned he.

As he passed out for the third time that day, Sir Hubris swore with all the angst of outraged youth he would denounce this fraud to the world.

§

"His Majesty is most pleased with the actions of his loyal servant," intoned the King's Seneschal as he pinned a bilious medal on Sir Hubris' chest.  There was also a leather purse which jingled in a most promising way.  "A small token of the Crown's appreciation.  For your expenses, of course," added the Seneschal with a knowing wink.

A passing trade caravan found him still hanging in the trees later that day, and carried him to the Lord's manor.  Several days of bed rest had Sir Hubris on the mend and he'd put the time to good use working himself up into a fine fury. He greeted the Seneschal's arrival with an enthusiasm the wolf pack would have appreciated, but this...well, this was completely unexpected. Sir Hubris didn't have two brain cells to rub together but he did have the peasant's low cunning, and right then it was telling him to keep his mouth shut and see how things broke.

Um, one exception on that: "You're too kind, your Excellency! I am unworthy of all this fuss!" Sucking up was part of the drill, then as always.

"True, but we can't have it said the Crown was ungracious."

"I'll be back on my feet in no time and ready to...ouch!..." He slumped back on the bed. His everything hurt. "...to return to duty."

"No hurry on that," grunted the Seneschal. "You're the Man Of The Hour, for the moment, and we'll be milking this for months to come. We'll be showing you to the bards and troubadours later in the day. You keep your mouth shut and suffer heroically," added he with a stern look. "I'll handle the PR!"

"Heroically, sir, yes, your Excellency! You can count on be to do my part for the cause!"

"Whatever."

Well: this left him in a quandary, to be sure! Duty done, the Seneschal beat a hasty retreat, leaving Sir Hubris to sort out the implications. No one *ever* accused him of being swift on the uptake, but he was beginning to realize he was a celebrity in the outing. And from what the Seneschal said, he ought to be able to "milk" this for a lot more than a measly sack of gold!

And then there was the big picture. As offended as he was by their duplicity, the Dragon Slayers' Order was all he had known in his young life. Revenge is sweet, yeah, but if he denounced the Order, he'd be out of a job. What alternative did he have: to become a city Guardsman?

"But I don't know any fine plump lassies!" moaned he.

§

The Elders of his Order came post-haste, incredulous at the news that one of their own had actually slain a dragon. Their reactions were predictable: "You don't expect us to believe you killed a Scottish dragon?" roared his Arms Master in derision. "What? Did it stumble over you and break it's neck? You don't even have the carcass to show!"

"Yeah!" yelled another Elder. "Where's the carcass, huh?"

"You're right, sir," said Sir Hubris. "I know it won't be easy to prove. The dragon said so himself. He said claims are often reconsidered even twenty years later if new evidence comes up." He gave the stump of the Arms Master's left arm pointed glance.

"Ummmm, well, speaking of that, the evidence is compelling if inconclusive," muttered his Arms Master, who realized which way the wind was blowing.

As to that evidence? Well, there were his multiple injuries and his tattered equipage, not to mention his lance—snapped off short and covered with dragon's blood. And there was the mangled hulk of poor Testosterone covered with, um, other evidence of the dragon. There was also the clearing trampled with the dragon's footsteps and more bloodstains and some loose scales from the monster's tail. Clearly this was the scene of a monumental battle!

"There is the proof, sirs," so claimed Sir Hubris.

"What other explanation is there?" said his Arms Master, pointedly.

"If he did, then I demand to see the carcass!" yelled one of the skeptical Elders.

"It must have crawled away to die. Dragons do that a lot, you know, and I for one am not going to go look for it. There are wolves in those woods!"

They argued the question at length, with the Arms Master offering the occasional well-timed remark and raised eyebrow so that by unspoken understanding they, too, soon came to know which way the wind was blowing. Inconclusive though the evidence was, there were bigger issues at stake here. The Elders weren't about to challenge his claim.

§

"Lor' bless ye, sir knight!" The villagers showed as much enthusiasm as they ever did when he returned to the School in honored procession. Dim-witted brutes, the lot of them, and he wondered if they had the better deal.

In the end, things worked out well for Sir Hubris. He was laid up in traction for over a year, then given a back brace and a teaching assignment since his dragon-slaying days were behind him. Today he limps around the training ground, barking instructions and handing out pushups with ruthless fury, hammering the young acolytes into shape for the challenges ahead.

Any doubts he entertained while hanging upside down from his saddle were soon buried by the relentless regimen, by liberal amounts of ale and by the perks of his new role as an Arms Master of the Dragon Slayers' Order. But sometimes, after his fourth or fifth mug, he wonders dimly just what did happen. Maybe he slew the dragon and maybe not. He'd lost consciousness several times, mumbles he into his cups, so there is no way of being sure what became of the creature. The memories are all so confusing.

"Whatever," sighs he.

And by the time his head drops on the inn table, the memories are dulled enough so when he wakes in the morning all that matters is—as a loyal member of the Order and an Arms Master at that— he *must* have slain the dragon, doubts or no. After all, isn't his bloody lance now enshrined as a holy Icon of the Order?

And if any of the acolytes has the wit to wonder if Sir Hubris knows what he's talking about, he often wakes up screaming, which soon convinces the worse doubters.

As for the dragon? Well, after the lance wound healed...but that's another story.

*****

# "A Rose By Any Other Name"

*Truly it is said that in the springtime of the year, the young maiden's thoughts turn to that most sacred of feminine duties, the finding of a suitable mate...*

*The Wise Teachings of V'ratheria*

§

"You sold me to that...that...*beast!*" Rose was appalled when her father informed her of the betrothal he had arranged. "Gracious Father, *why?*"

Rose always was a wayward child, but her father was troubled enough that he didn't rebuke her for questioning him. "One *hopes* it shall be a blessed union," he murmured. "Being the Warlord's concubine is a rare honor..."

Rose was distraught by then. "Rare honor? How many young maidens has he gone through?"

"It was...necessary...to assure your family's position in the court..."

Her father was a minor functionary in the Warlord's palace and, like all such, both constantly struggled for favor and constantly feared his Master's displeasure. Moves like this were all too common. Rose was born into what until then had seemed a charmed life. It was only recently, as she blossomed into her maturity, she began to hear hints of the dire fate of many such daughters. She dismissed them in the past as lurid rumor or juicy gossip, but now she faced those rumors head on. She was dismayed, nay, terrified.

"*Necessary?* How could you *do* such a thing to your own flesh and blood?" With that she fled to her room in tears.

Her Gracious Mother was equally appalled by the news, but was steeped enough in tradition that she kept her peace. She and their maidservant sorrowed as they bathed her and dressed her in her favorite dancers' costume. She loved to dance to the beat of drums and tambourines, to their frequent dismay, but now they felt it was her one hope. "You can only pray the Warlord enjoys you," her mother said. "We know so *little* of his tastes, so you must be prepared for anything."

"*How* could father do this to me?" she cried.

"It is the fate of women," her mother said, sadly. "The Warlord commands, and you must be prepared to serve His whims."

Despite her woebegone state, she was ravishing: tall, slim, narrow-waisted, with flowing dark hair and almond eyes now red with tears. She was quick-witted and willful, and her parents sometimes despaired of her ever becoming a proper wife. Who would take someone so outspoken? It didn't matter now: as concubine to the Warlord, her future was as certain as it was bound to be brief. Far more tractable maidens had gone to His harem—never to be seen again.

It was midday when an escort from the palace Mamluks came for her. Her father was away attending court, so her mother was the only one to see her off. "Bless you, my child," she said, sorrowfully.

"Gracious Mother..."

"Go, child." Her mother kissed her forehead and hugged her close with tears in her eyes. "May the Gods grant you peace."

Her escort was an unfortunate choice under the circumstances. Ulmac was recently enrolled in the Mamluks, and was everything her girlish fantasies could want. She had flirted with him on many occasions, drawn by his tall stature and athletic build, and he proved receptive to her charms. They even exchanged a furtive kiss now and then, and it was understood without saying that he would speak to her father soon. Then this tragic turn came to pass. He was no less stricken than her, but had no choice but to do his assigned duties, though it grated on him.

"Please, Ulmac!" she pleaded with him as he escorted her across the square. "Don't take me there! You know I love you; help me escape."

Ulmac's jaw muscles twitched with his tension, and his hand tightened on his sword. "Would that I could, my love," he said, sorrowfully. "But there is nothing I can do. The gates are too well guarded, and I cannot get you past them."

"I thought you loved me!"

"I do, my precious, but what can a mere man do?"

§

All too soon they arrived at the service gate leading to the inner palace. Ulmac produced a key, unlocked the gate, and reluctantly coaxed her in. She hesitated for a long moment then, resigned to her fate, stepped through.

Ulmac gave her one last sorrowful look after he pulled the gate shut. "I must go now. His Radiance is dispensing justice, so I must attend to my duties." He glanced around furtively, then gave her a hasty kiss through the bars. "Good by," he murmured. "I'm sorry." He turned and walked away, his shoulders drooped in dejection as Rose clung to the bars.

She stood there for some time, clinging to the gate, sobbing softly. Many were the attractive young maidens who came through this gate; few if any were ever seen again. She'd heard the dreadful rumors of what became of them, and her heart was filled with terror and despair. She bitterly cursed her Gracious Father who sold her to a dreadful fate to insure his own position, and prayed that he suffer a similar fate.

"Ahem!"

It was the Castellan: a dandy fellow, tall and thin, dressed in a colorful toga of decidedly feminine cut with his bejeweled collar of office overall. She knew him from a distance since childhood, and always thought there was something *odd* about him. For one, he had the peculiar habit of referring to himself in the third person. That overwhelming perfume didn't help, either. He looked her over with a disdainful sniff. "Another one for the dogs. Pity."

That confirmed her worst fears. "Please!" she pleaded with him. "Can you help me?" For all his effeminate ways, he was a power in the inner court, and not someone to cross. "I beg of you! Spare me this fate!"

He gave her a chilly look. "His Excellency, the Castellan is a loyal servant to His Radiance, and would never *think* of going against His will. Your fate is sealed, child. You belong to the Warlord, and you must make the best of it. If you can."

"Save me from him!" she begged. "I shall be yours, willingly!"

"His Excellency, the Castellan, is sensible enough not to covet that belonging to His Radiance. In any event, he has six pretties already, and he thinks you not the sort for his bed."

He gripped her arm and half-dragged her through narrow back corridors deep into the palace, up several flights of stairs which emptied into a broad hall which lead in turn to the gate of the harem. Another key gained entrance, and she was shoved in unceremoniously. "His Radiance is attending to court," he said after pulling the gate shut and locking it again. "You have until this evening to compose yourself."

He left her then, and she looked around frantically for some improbable escape. The harem was like something out of a romantic fantasy, not that she appreciated its beauty. It had a high, arched ceiling with golden lanterns suspended. The walls were decorated with lovely tapestries between high windows of multi-colored glass. The floor was polished marble of many hues, covered with furs and woven rugs. There were several ornate fountains, a large bath, and sumptuous downy beds piled with silken pillows. The place was empty other than her, although large enough for a dozen or more, and she caught the implications at once.

She ran to an open doorway where sunlight poured through, and found herself on a balcony overlooking the ornamental gardens. The inner wall of the palace rose nearly to her height opposite, with the Mamluk duty watch pacing their rounds. Beyond were the towers of the outer wall, which she had never ventured past in her young life, and beyond those the mountains filled the horizon with gray and glistening white. A trellis, bedecked with flowers, climbed the wall around her. Many songbirds nested in those flowery heights and filled the air with their song. It was a lovely, surreal scene, but one she could hardly appreciate in her present state. There was no escape. Even if she survived the jump, she could never climb over those walls.

*THONK!* A heavy noise in the distance was answered by a rising wail of distraught voices. That distracted her, and she looked around to see where it came from. To her left, between the entrance and the balcony, was an open area with a railing. *THONK!* Another surge of anguish. She didn't want to know what that was about, but she was drawn to the opening in spite of herself.

The opening proved to be a small balcony overlooking the court; a splendor of this world with its vast polished marble floor, its gilded pillars and its walls lined with woven tapestries. But all she saw was the horror in its center.

The Warlord sat upon His bejeweled throne high above the ranked courtiers. Before Him sat the chopping block, with the hooded headsman resting on his ax. There was blood everywhere: a great pool of it around the block, a smeared trail where the corpses of the condemned were dragged away, splatters on everything. A woven basket by the block held the severed heads. In the background stood a herd of chained prisoners guarded by the palace Mamluks. As she watched in horror, two of them dragged another prisoner from the crowd and forced him to kneel in the bloody pool before the block.

*THONK!* She cringed at the sound of the headman's ax and the rising murmur of the crowd, and stared transfixed by the spreading pool of blood before His throne. Two Mamluks dragged the corpse to one side while two more dragged the next victim before Him.

She retreated then, too appalled for words, threw herself on a bed and buried her head under the pillows. *THONK!* The wails of lamentation from the condemned were matched by her whimper of terror as she clung to the pillow and tried futilely to shut out the world.

*THONK!* The executions went on relentlessly. *THONK!* The Warlord's wrath was well known throughout His empire... *THONK!* He was all too ready to lop off heads, hands, feet, genitals... *THONK!* Justice was swift and brutal under His reign... *THONK!*

At that, beheading was merciful. *THONK!* Many were sent to the salt mines, and those who truly earned His wrath endured the most horrid fate...*THONK!*...being thrown to the ravenous hunting dogs, who were never fed otherwise.

*THONK!* She cringed with each new stroke of the headsman's ax. *THONK!* The crowd wailed. He must be in a grim mood that day. *THONK!* Her fearful imagination was overwhelmed with the horrors awaiting her when He came for her. *THONK!*...

§

Eventually—she lost track of the time, cowering in the mass of pillows—the heavy thuds of the headsman's ax and the diminishing wails of the condemned faded. Silence returned, broken only by the trickling of the fountains and the trilling of the songbirds outside, and by her morbid terror.

She was shaken out of her despair by the grating of the gate lock. When she looked up, night had fallen. The Warlord stood before her. He was shorter than she thought, no taller than her, but immensely fat, with puffy cheeks and multiple chins. For all His bulk, His arms were thin and flabby, and seemed even smaller compared to His sagging belly. He was dressed in His robes of State; the pantaloons and velvet slippers were soaked in blood; the throne room must be a charnel house.

She scrambled to her feet, and stood nervously before Him, trying hard to hold onto her composure, which was made even harder by the whip in His pudgy hand. What did He intend to do with that? The horrid rumors of the fate of His prior conquests flitted through her mind, driving her to the edge of panic.

Then, without speaking, He opened His robe and threw it off, exposing His pale belly. He pulled at His waistband and slid the pantaloons down, finally kicking them and the blood soaked slippers off. She stood stock still, fighting the urge to scream; to run; to hurl herself on Him scratching and biting. The sight of His wallowing nakedness was utterly revolting, so much so that she believed being fed to the dogs was more merciful.

He stood before her gazing into her eyes for a long moment, then held the whip out with both hands. "I w-want your love," He squeaked.

That shook her out of her trance. "M-my Lord...?"

He pressed the whip into her hands, then sank to His knees, kneeling before her. "S-show m-me how you l-love me."

The sight of Him kneeling before her—what disgusting unnatural act did He intend for her?—was more than she could bear. The sight of His quivering pallid flab and the thought of Him venting His lust upon her innocent body was sickening. "I...no...I can't..."

He looked up at her and frowned. "Love me, wench!"

It was too much. Her self-control collapsed, and she shoved Him away. "Y-you *beast!* You vile monster!" She was doomed and knew it, and with that all her pent up angst came boiling out of her in an uncontrollable rush. "You're disgusting!" She raised the whip again and again, thrashing His broad back without willing it, completely out of control. "S-send me to the dogs! I don't care! I'd rather *die* than have you touch me!"

Finally her rage evaporated; she threw the whip at Him and ran for a remote corner, bawling in shame and disgust.

§

The Castellan found her the next morning sunk in despair in a fetal curl where she had cried herself to sleep in a far corner of the harem. "The sun is in the heavens and you are still a-bed? It seems your lot is not so bad as feared."

"He'll have me killed!" she whimpered. "He'll throw me to the dogs!"

"If that were so, He would not order breakfast sent to you."

"What?" She stirred in surprise, and rolled over just as a servant set a tray by her bed and removed the cover, revealing an abundance of fruits and sweetmeats.

"This is a rare occasion indeed, one worthy of celebration. His Excellency congratulates you on surviving the night."

"But...I refused Him," she murmured in confusion. "I disobeyed...I...I struck Him..."

"Indeed you did."

"A-and He *forgave* me?" This simply didn't jibe with the massacre in the throne room earlier. "H-he's not going to throw me to the dogs?"

"Do not despair...yet. His Radiance said you are the first concubine in some years who showed any spark at all."

"But...I don't understand..."

The Castellan smiled knowingly. "You are young, and have much to learn about the wicked ways of the world." Her obvious confusion earned a derisive snort. "It is said that great men, men of power and wealth, often secretly crave relief from their feelings of inadequacy."

"In...adequacy?"

46

"His Radiance is a man of vast power, yet as you no doubt saw..." He mused for a bit. "One might say He lacks the martial qualities of His forbearers, which plagues Him with self-doubt and self-loathing."

"But..."

"Truth, His greatest frustration is His magnificence. All who come before Him, including the many maidens taken as concubines, are overawed. Such fawning deference leaves Him...unfulfilled...bitter..."

"But...me?"

"You indeed." The Castellan gave her a knowing look. "For the first time in years He has found relief from His self-loathing through your abuse and debasement. Discreet inquiries show you were always a willful child. It may yet be your salvation."

"He...enjoyed...?"

"His Excellency, the Castellan, has not seen Him in such a fine mood for some time. He understands there are to be only half the usual executions today."

He bowed to her and left her there wondering at this strange turn of fate. He *wanted* her to reject Him? To whip Him? Rose had never heard of the like, but it must be true, else she would be in the kennels by now. Then she noticed the bowl in front of her, and helped herself to a date. Perhaps she would live after all.

§

She was more or less composed by that evening, having spent the day pondering this odd situation. Honestly, she wasn't sure how to proceed. She had been approached by many would-be lovers in her time, but always sent them away gently. Even at her tender age, she knew one could never be sure if a rejected suitor might prove useful later. But this situation was completely outside her experience, and honestly made no sense. She knew people who enjoyed inflicting pain, but the idea of receiving pain willingly, even craving it, was beyond her.

But this was no time to ponder human folly. She was in mortal danger, and if her path to survival was to abuse and debase Him, then she needed to get past her squeamishness and deliver. Even better, if He craved rejection, then she could hold Him at bay; the thought of enduring His lust was sickening. The only problem was she wasn't sure how to do it without pushing Him into His all-too-murderous rage. She was balanced on a knife edge; the Gods must be laughing their fool heads off at this odd twist of fate, but she couldn't count on them to save her if she made a misstep. She wasn't sure how far to go, or what might set Him off; a delicate balancing act indeed, yet she had no choice but to play the game.

The Warlord found her in this optimistic mood when He came for her that evening. As before, she stood when He entered and awaited His next move. As before, He carried a whip. As before, He glared at her, then shed His clothes and approached her, His flabby belly and thighs wobbling. At last He stood before her and looked her over while she wondered anxiously what to do next.

"I t-trust you a-p-preciate my finer qualities this evening," He said, timidly. "Love me, girl."

Acting on impulse—she had nothing to lose—she stuck out her hand. "Give me that!" she snapped. After a tense moment, He handed the whip to her. She hefted it, bemused by its weight, then looked Him over with heart-felt disgust. "I suppose You expect me to swoon in Your arms?"

His expression darkened. "I e-expect you t-to be a p-proper harem girl."

"Do you now?"

If this was an act, His glowering look was all too convincing. She needed to do something before His patience wore thin. She hefted the whip and flicked in tentatively, then wound up and threw an all-out long arm lash as she had seen used for flogging common miscreants in the public square. To her surprise, the whip made a resounding *CRACK!* He stared at it, and whimpered...

§

Life went on amid the daily routine of the palace. Ulmac carried out his duties with grim, unsociable determination while the Mamluks gossiped in wonder. His love for the now-departed Rose was common knowledge, and his superiors worried he might do something rash. Nonetheless, he was shaping up into an outstanding warrior; fit, disciplined, hard working, always ready for any task. While his leaders worried about him, they also followed his progress with approval. As a test, he was given a Second's armband and a sliver of authority, hoping the prospect of promotion would snap him out of his longing. He rose to that challenge like he did all such; by making it look easy. As was custom, he was soon assigned to the inner palace wall, a mark of distinction among the Mamluks.

It was on a mild spring day a few weeks after Rose entered the harem, that she appeared on a balcony. She was wrapped in a colorful robe, and stood for some time, gazing forlornly out over the ornamental gardens to the mountains on the horizon. Ulmac recognized her in the distance as he patrolled his station on the palace wall, and the sight tore at him. *Mercifully* she was still alive, although she doubtlessly endured the torments of the damned as the object of the Warlord's lust. She turned and disappeared into the harem, leaving him bereft.

He longed for her, and cursed his weakness at not finding a way to spare her when she begged him to, and renewed his vow to rescue her somehow. Still, despite his superiors' concern, he knew better than to place his life, and hers, at risk by a rash move. So he walked his post, and cursed the Warlord, and pondered his options, and waited for the right moment...

§

"Ow! Mph! Easy there!" She shook off the Warlord's masseur, a brutish oaf with all the touch of a bull wrestler, and sat up on her couch. "Where did you learn your trade? In the stables? I swear you're bruising me!"

The masseur was righteously offended. "I have served His Radiance since before you were born," he said, sternly. "He is satisfied by my labors, and you should be grateful He commanded me to serve you as well!"

"Grateful? Being fed to the dogs holds no terrors after you!"

"You are an ungracious wench! I do not see what He finds so attractive about you!"

That got her temper up. "Why don't you ask Him if you're so curious?" He pulled in his horns abruptly, knowing full well the fate of anyone who questioned the Warlord's actions. "Perhaps I shall ask Him to explain it to you. Would you like me to do that?"

He buckled under the threat. "You are not long for His favor," he muttered as he retreated. "They never last, and I don't expect you to either."

"Don't count on it!" she swore as he left.

§

The days past as spring turned into summer. The crops were planted, and the weather turned warmer and dryer. The harem, which was comfortable enough in the spring, soon became stifling.

"Can't you do something?" she asked the Castellan. "If you could have some of these windows taken out, the breeze would be a blessing."

"The Castellan regrets that would be difficult," he said. "His Radiance spent a fortune to decorate this place, and He would have to approve any changes."

"Isn't there something you can do?" she pleaded. "I would be most grateful."

The Castellan mused for a bit, looking her over speculatively. "One *supposes* certain of those windows could be removed for repair, which might take all summer. The Castellan would love to attend to that, but his days are occupied with matters of court, alas. Perhaps once His Radiance gives His assent to certain laws..."

She caught his drift at once. "How soon can you have those windows removed?"

The Castellan smiled.

§

"I am told Morngravian incense is all but impossible to obtain," she told the Warlord that evening. "Apparently bandits are pillaging the caravans. Can't You do something? Send an escort, or post a garrison somewhere?"

"You too?" He muttered. "M-my Castellan annoys Me by n-night and by day. Little d-does he think of the cost..."

"As well he should, as should You!" She stood before the kneeling Warlord and rapped His forehead smartly with the butt of her whip. "Your duty is to protect the merchants." She forced His flabby face up to focus His gaze right into her cleavage. "And I *love* Morngravian incense. Is that asking so much?"

The Warlord sighed. "So it s-shall be, M-my precious."

That went easier than expected, and it seemed earning the Castellan's favor could pay handsomely. This opened up some interesting prospects. She returned to pacing in a circle around Him where He knelt before her couch, her contempt plain with every gesture.

"And while you're at it, the only person I see here is You, which is hardly pleasant company. I am lonely and bored. I want You to provide me a handmaiden...two handmaidens, and a better masseur as well."

"I s-shall send you two handm-maidens, My precious, b-but I cannot replace My m-masseur. He is an old established m-member of My court, and I c-cannot toss him aside."

She stopped in front of Him and gave Him a stern look. "Court intrigue, I take it?" There was nothing for it, and this was distracting them from the flow of events. "Very well, if You *cannot* command Your own court, I shall expect the two handmaidens at least." She snapped the whip near His face. "Promptly!"

"I s-shall make it s-so, M-my precious."

§

In the meanwhile, Ulmac received a stroke of fortune long sought: one of the junior Beys died from drinking tainted wine, and Ulmac soon came to his superiors' attention as they pondered a replacement. His record thus far was exemplary, so he received the late Bey's baton and command of two hands of men. His fellow Mamluks applauded this despite the unusual speed of his promotion, which also brought about a shift to the night watch. It was the break he'd been looking for.

He had not forgotten his pledge to save Rose. She was rightfully his—did she not made her interest plain?—and a *man* stands up for what is rightfully his, especially his woman. As things came together, he began formulating a plan to rescue her. It galled him to think of her enduring His vile passions, submitting out of mortal fear, suffering the shame and revulsion of His revolting pleasures. Yes, soon he would rescue his beloved, and end her dark nightmare...

§

"That masseur is a clumsy oaf," Rose complained a few days later while the pleasant breeze fanned her hair. "This morning he gave me two more bruises! Can't you do something with him?"

The Warlord was kneeling by her bedside, and offered her another fig. "There now, My dear. P-pray not b-be angry with him. H-he is f-from an old f-family of m-my strongest l-loyalists. I d-dare not send him t-to the mines. W-what can I do?"

She figured as much some time ago. She sighed theatrically and caressed her bare thigh with an ostrich feather, evoking a whimper from Him. "Still, I wish you could think of something." That oaf was becoming an obsession with her.

His hand slipped from the bowl by her bedside, and one finger furtively touched the hem of her bodice. She slapped His hand smartly. "Another grape, please."

§

Having finished his rounds, Ulmac paused on the inner wall and gazed longingly at the balcony where he got occasional glimpses of his beloved Rose. The balcony was highlighted by the golden rays of sunset which sparkled and danced on the colored glass windows. But there was no sight of her. She seldom came to the balcony any more, which worried him. Was she so sunken in shame and despair that she had lost the will to live?

He was torn by the thought of her; thankfully the Warlord spared her thus far, but he was anguished by their separation and the cruel fate which befell her. He spent practically every waking hour thinking of how to rescue her, and while he found nothing yet, his posting to the night watch opened up all *sorts* of possibilities. Once more he cursed the Warlord and the ill turn of fate which kept him from protecting his beloved, as a man should. Hopefully he could find something before her misery and hopelessness drove her to some fatal error.

§

The Warlord came to her in the evening after court, as usual, and as usual He brought her a gift. "I h-had t-this made f-for you, My precious," He stammered as a servant held it up for her to see. It was a mesh gown of fine golden chain, picked out here and there with rubies and emeralds, with a gold collar of inlaid filigree.

She was thrilled. "It's beautiful!" Without a second thought, she shed her velvet gown and slipped it over her head. It weighed as only real gold can. The weight made it cling to her, accenting all and concealing nothing as she admired herself in the large mirror. She had never seen anything quite so *scandalous* before, and was delighted by how it hugged her curves. "The court jewelers have outdone themselves this time..." She glanced at Him...and noticed how He was responding to her sensual nakedness. That worried her; He'd never done *that* before...

In a sudden impulse, she kicked Him right where it counted. He folded up on the floor, clutching Himself. "Don't you *dare* raise like that to me again!" she said, coldly. She went back to admiring herself in the mirror, secretly appalled at what she'd done. For all the abuse she endured upon Him, there had to be some limit she dared not cross. Had she pushed Him too far? All she could do was remain calm and try to bluff her way out of any reaction on His part. One of her serving maids brought her favorite robe which she donned to cover herself, but held it open so she could study herself in the mirror. "This *is* lovely. Thank you."

"I am...g-glad you l-like it," He wheezed as He struggled to His knees.

*Mercifully*, it seemed she hadn't reached His limits...yet. She gave Him a stern look, then settled on her favorite couch, arraying herself so her gown fell carelessly open. If He would take that, He would take anything she cared to dish out. This opened up all *sorts* of possibilities.

"Now, let us review Your decisions in the court today." She smiled as she picked up the whip and toyed with it. "Hopefully Your reign has improved since You were here last?"

§

By high summer, the executions had dwindled to a rare few, the hunting dogs often went hungry, and the salt mines were begging for labor. The courtiers remarked to each other about how relaxed and even *mellow* the Warlord was those days. People throughout the Empire marveled at this change, wondering why His Radiance showed such unexpected mercy. One notable exception was Rose's Gracious Father, who was summarily thrown to the dogs for reasons no one could see. The courtiers took that philosophically; the dogs had to be fed *sometime*, cattle were expensive, and it was just so much less competition for them.

Ulmac went about his duties with grim, tight-lipped precision. His superiors' earlier fears about him had faded, and he was starting to be noticed for his prowess as a warrior. He was promoted to Ghilman and given command of a section of the wall, and he continued to be a strict and exacting disciplinarian. His men cursed his relentless driving will, but were secretly proud of how they stood out among the palace Mamluks.

And all the while he agonized over his beloved Rose. She came to the balcony less and less frequently of late, but she seemed to be well. The occasional sight of her was a dagger in his heart, and he swore vengeance to the Warlord...and swore to redeem himself as a man...and plotted...

§

The late summer Jade Festival was in full swing, and the Warlord was busy holding court (which didn't involve bloodshed, for once). Since He was occupied, Rose took the occasion for a long, luxurious bath followed by the ministrations of her new hairdresser. She reclined on her favorite couch and indulged in a bunch of grapes while the chamber musicians played something relaxing in the background. The steady stroke of the hairbrush was hypnotic, and she floated in a blissful half-doze.

Her peaceful reverie was broken by the rattle of the harem gate. "What does *He* want?" she grumbled. The Warlord appeared, but before He could speak, she looked Him over with obvious impatience. "I am busy. You shall have to come back some other time."

"B-but I w-want..."

"I have no time for You now!" she snapped. "You may go."

The Warlord stared at her in dismay. Their eyes met and she glared at Him, then He averted His gaze and left.

"You take a terrible risk, my Lady," her hairdresser said, earnestly. "By all accounts His wrath is fearful."

She smiled at her. "You don't know Him as I do, Aasha."

§

The harvests were taken in due season, and the harvest festivals were lighter and gayer than in years past. The common herd were less restive than ever, and the daily floggings often had a festive atmosphere.

Within the palace, the courtiers acted as if a tremendous burden long borne—a burden of fear—had been lifted from them. The palace celebration was lively, with the Warlord in attendance along with His harem favorite who lead Him about on a golden chain. It was *quite* the scandal, and the courtiers teetered and snickered at the sight. That young wench not only survived, but somehow gained His favor to *such* a degree that He allowed her this *outré* privilege.

Later that evening several new laws were announced at the court, some of which surprised those in attendance. Since when did His Radiance concern Himself with economic matters? Or limits on floggings? Or, especially, the rights of women? They shook their heads, mystified, and went back to drinking.

Life among the Mamluks was peasant in that time. Palace security was less concerned about a peasant uprising than ever, and the night watch, now commanded by Ulmac, could relax their vigilance. And all the while he watched the distant balcony, and fumed...waiting for just the right moment. The time was near: the Gods must smile upon the two of them to allow so many coincidences to pass. His plans were complete, and all which remained now was to set them in motion.

The big question—how to get her beyond the walls—was finally resolved. A length of stout rope would free her from the harem, and his recently granted set of keys would get her out of the palace. They would need a means to escape: there were fine horses in the palace stables, and he had gathered supplies from the palace stores. Yes, everything was ready; soon he would claim Rose as his dutiful and loving wife. It required many measures which needed discretion, but since he could arrange the night watch...

§

There came a moonless night when a chill autumn fog shrouded the palace grounds and muffled any random noises. A furtive figure emerged from a storeroom, looked all about, then crept across the courtyard. A key was produced, opening the secure passageway into the garden. Once inside, at the base of the wall, the figure hefted a rope over one shoulder and carefully scaled the trellis...

§

The Warlord was kneeling naked before her in the center of the harem, while she was dressed in her favorite, scantiest costume of fine golden chain and little else. She was about to speak to when she caught a movement out of the corner of her eye.

"*Ulmac?*"

She and the Warlord both stepped back in surprise, and the Warlord was about to shout for the watch when Ulmac put sword to His throat; He froze in fear, eyes bulging.

"Ulmac, my beloved!" She was thrilled to see him up close again, which evoked her all but forgotten girlish fantasies. "You came to rescue me? You came to sweep me up in your *manly* arms and bear me away?"

"I have, my beloved." He eyed the Warlord's revolting nakedness with obvious disgust. "This vile creature shall defile you no more!"

"But you shall be killed!"

He shook his head as he kept the Warlord at bay. "There are two swift steeds ready by the south postern gate, which is unguarded this night. We can outrun any pursuit, and vanish into the hinterlands."

She could see all sorts of problems with that, not the least of which being she had never ridden a horse. Trust a *man* not to think of those things. "But surely we cannot remain in this land? We shall be hunted by the Mamluks."

"We must flee to the hills. It shall be a harsh life, but you shall be free, and we shall be together."

"Free? In the hills?" Winter was coming on.

"In the farthest reaches, where none may find us."

"Living with you in some cave?" That wasn't promising.

"I shall save you from this decadence, my love. I have my bow to take game for food and clothing. It shall make us strong for our lives ahead."

Give up her downy bed? "You would dress me in hides?"

"There are many deer in the hills, fat from the summer's grazing. Their pelts are thick this time of year."

"I am to cook over an open fire?" She always *hated* cooking.

"If that be our lot, then we shall endure for our love."

"If that be our lot..."

"And in the spring, after the hunt has died down, we shall make our way to foreign lands, where I can find service as a mercenary. We shall travel the world together, living the free soldier's life."

"The life of a soldier's wife?" All of a sudden this didn't seem so romantic.

"Indeed, my love." He looked her up and down, noting her skimpy costume with obvious interest. "And we shall have many fine sons, as befits a great man and great warrior."

"I am to bear you many sons?" She never thought about that before. No, this didn't sound so romantic at all.

"Many fine sons indeed, my love." He gave the Warlord a murderous glare. "But first you shall die, you revolting worm!" He hefted his sword and advanced on the Warlord, who backed away in terror. "You shall pay for your vile debasement of this virtuous maiden..."

There was a sickening thud, and Ulmac collapsed in a heap at the Warlord's feet. Rose stood behind him holding a heavy flower pot. "Well?" she said as the Warlord looked on in dismay. "Don't just stand there. Call the watch!"

§

It was some time before Ulmac came to, only to find himself bound hand and foot, surrounded by the duty watch and most of the courtiers. No sooner did he awaken then he was hauled to his feet before the Warlord now hastily dressed in a nightshirt.

"You t-t-treacherous c-cur!" The Warlord was beside himself in rage. "Y-you b-betrayed me!"

"Would that I *killed* you!" Ulmac spat in His face.

"T-take him away!" the Warlord squeaked. "C-castrate him! Throw him t-to the dogs!"

"NO!" The Warlord cringed under her outburst as Rose stepped between them. "You must not harm him!"

"Rose? I'm sorry, my love."

"I'm sorry too, Ulmac, my love, but I couldn't let you take me away from this." She gestured around the sumptuous bedchamber.

"Rose? You...?" He stared at her in confusion.

"That was naughty of you, but I forgive you. You are such a big, strong, *virile* man; how could I not forgive you?" She kissed him languorously as the Warlord moaned in dismay. Ulmac might yet serve a useful purpose... "I suppose I shall *always* love you and the many fine sons we might have had." The Warlord was sniveling. "But my place is here now, my love."

She turned to the Castellan, who was eying Ulmac speculatively. "I believe you have six pretties for your bed?"

The Castellan's lips twitched with a hint of a smile. "Indeed, the Castellan said as much some time ago."

"Now you have seven." Ulmac and the Warlord both squawked in disbelief while the Castellan chuckled and bowed to her. Favor received would be favor repaid, later. Meanwhile, it was time to set matters to rest once and for all. "And since you are here, I shall require a *proper* masseur, one who won't leave me bruised and sore." She waved contemptuously at the present masseur, hovering in a corner. "Send *that* buffoon to the dungeons to learn how to serve his Radiance *properly*. If he doesn't meet my exacting standards, he can be fed to the dogs for all I care."

"Ah...but his family..."

"Shall have no objections, since his position is secure. *Assuming* he proves capable of the honor."

"So it shall be, Your Radiance," the Castellan said with an unabashed grin.

"But...but...but..." The Warlord was distraught as the guards dragged Ulmac away. "He b-broke into the harem! H-he t-tried to k-kill me!"

She spun and confronted him, hands on hips. "YOU! Be silent and fetch me wine! Saving your sorry hide is thirsty work."

The Warlord wilted visibly. "Yes, my Lady," he whimpered as he scuttled to do Her bidding.

*****

## "Even Wizards Have Bad Days"

"It's such a nice day outside," Ja-moke the Green said, hopefully. "Do you really have to destroy the world today?"

Mal-binizar the Black paused to sneer at him. "And what do I care for the world? It'll be a nicer day once I get through with it!"

Ja-moke shrugged. "You say so. It just seems a shame, is all."

§

*Mal-binizar the Black was a power-obsessed monster utterly devoted to the pursuit of the darkest, most dreadful forbidden knowledge and his own promotion thereby; not the sort who gets invited to tea in polite circles. He was tall and angular, with a high forehead and narrow shoulders, and he seemed rather pathetic until you saw the feverish gleam in his eyes. One could say he had issues.*

*Right then he was fiddling with the wand of now-former fellow mage Bel-ama the Purple, who came to a gristly end thanks to Mal-binizar a couple hours earlier. At that, he, Mal-binizar, lucked out: it was a near-run thing.*

*Perhaps the best description for Mal-binizar was 'dangerous fool', though not many would offer that opinion to his face no matter how widely held. People who take up Black magic are usually described as "obsessive" or "antisocial" or "psychotic" or all three; the sort who thrash recklessly forth where demons fear to tread. Mal-binizar in particular was a name whispered...usually while trying to keep a straight face. Anyone who plunged whole-heartedly into the Black Arts like he did, and survived as long as he had, was not to be taken lightly. The fact that many did smirk at the mention of his name proves that 'greatest' does not necessarily equate with 'best'; rather more like 'luckiest'.*

§

"This seems awfully risky," Ja-moke said. "There are so many things which can go wrong tampering with another mage's wand. Wouldn't it be better to get the Old Ones to do this for you?"

§

*Ja-moke the Green, on the other hand, was a bald, rotund little man with a placid, likable nature. Green magic was the realm of the Fertility Goddess, and she had a thing for bald, rotund little men. He loved nothing more than working the growing and flowering spells to insure a bountiful crop, and his favorite holiday was the annual harvest bacchanal. (The Goddess insured not every part of him was short, bless her fertility-obsessed heart.) They were an unlikely pair which left a lot of people wondering, but in fact he had devoted himself in self-preservation to talking Mal-Binizar down from some of his more dastardly —and erratic—schemes. Frankly, he was hoping the Old Ones would seize the wand, and perhaps Mal-binizar as well, if given the chance.*

§

Mal-binizar favored him with a chilly glare. "I dueled with Bel-ama the Purple for forty-seven porkin' *years* to get this blasted wand, and by all that's unholy, I intend to put it to good use!"

"Yes, but the Old Ones..."

"In the first place, the Old Ones demand their price, and the price they'd demand for this is more than I care to pay. And in the second place, I *doubt* they will want to exalt me as supreme above them, so it's unlikely they'd be willing to unlock this wand for me anyway."

"Oh." Nice try.

§

*Any realm of magic has its risks, but the Black Arts are especially not for the faint of heart. It's no surprise 99 out of 100 wind up dead in wonderfully messy and painful ways, but there are worse things then dying for the few who last long enough to become really proficient. Not many do, but if you are going to pity a Black mage, save it for those poor fools who botch an evocation of the Old Ones. Slur a syllable when evoking Rott-t-th-zidxnd-bhhuth-rineggnxgi-Homag or Gixxnjiii-ag-hro-nag-hnaar-ragxxoroth, and your last horrified shriek will haunt the spot you stood on for centuries to come. No, the Black Arts are left strictly alone by anyone with any sense at all, which didn't include Mal-binizar the Black.*

§

"And don't go name-dropping you-know-who like that," he lectured Ja-moke. "You don't want to get their attention by mistake."

"Um...sorry."

"Now *if* you don't mind, I'm busy trying to override this identity lock. This is delicate work, and I *don't* need to be disturbed while fooling with this much power. So put a sock in it for a while!"

§

*His caution (albeit late in the day, considering) was understandable. Wands gain in power with time and use. Any piece of wood can be oriented into a wand, but a new one won't do much more than stir dust or kill a fly. Mal-binizar's wand had been in heavy use for over 800 years, and could blast huge craters in the face of the moon. The only other wand coming close to that was Bel-ama the Purple's, having been in steady use for over 650 years.*

§

"Um..."

"WHAT?" Mal-binizar about jumped out of his skin, and rounded on Ja-moke in a rage. "Perhaps I should turn you into a toad for a while to shut you up? Toads are green, and you look like a toad to start with!"

"Sorry. I was just going to urge you to be careful."

§

*Anyway: wands amplify the power of a spell. One conjures a spell, and the wand amplifies it and shoots it in the direction aimed. Point your finger and if you're good, you can drop an opponent at close range. Use Mal-binizar's wand and whole regions could be depopulated. As dreadful as that sounds, spells are normally small stuff compared to evocations. But Mal-binizar intended to try something novel, and amazingly stupid...*

§

"Let — me — see..." he muttered as he examined the wand. "Touch here, and here...evoke Ka'broth'mugga (mumbling while consulting a scroll of Purple spells). Solve the riddle...and...Yyyeeessssssss!" He straightened up with an air of self-satisfaction, twirled the wand between his fingers like a baton, then fired a stream of multicolored sparks into the air. "Done!"

"Huzzah," Ja-moke mumbled.

"Now I can cast my *ultimate* vampire spell! Using Bel-ama's wand and amplifying it through my wand will give me the ultimate power in the Universe!"

*Not* good. "But can you control so much power? Either wand is a hideous weapon in its own right, but their combined power should equal a wand half a million years old!"

"EX-actly! Can you *imagine* the result?"

"Yes. The earth could shatter under the impact!"

"Then I'll rebuild it after I absorb the life essence of *every living thing*, including the Old Ones themselves."

"I really don't see what good it will do to become an Old One if there's nothing left." Ja-moke never gave up reasoning with Mal-binizar, forlorn hope that it was. "What will you do with no worshipers to fear you?"

"Don't sweat the petty things," Mal-binizar sneered. "I'll create my own race of worshipers later. And I'll thank you to *butt out* for once, and leave Doomsday to me!"

"I'm just trying to help," Ja-moke muttered, despondently.

§

*Thus the thankless life of trying to contain Mal-binizar's destructive impulses. Ja-moke worked his way into Mal-binizar's trust—as much as anyone could—decades ago expressly to tamp him down as needed; he wouldn't have anything to do with a Black mage otherwise. Mal-Binizar evidently never saw through his little schemes since his tall, commanding presence (in his own eyes, anyway) rated a goofy sidekick. Little did he know Ja-moke would gladly run a shiv between his ribs of he could, or that the Gods would appreciate the favor.*

§

"You know, it's a shame about Atlantis." Ja-moke was nothing if not persistent. "I know you aren't much of a people person, but the city itself is rather nice. D'you suppose maybe you could arrange for them to be left out of your Armageddon?"

"They are ants to me," Mal-binizar sneered. He sneered a lot. "Less than ants. If anything, I do them an undeserved favor, for they won't be around to witness my wrath and majesty!"

"You say so."

"Yes, I say so. Now all that remains is to set up the spell, and my life's ambition will be achieved!"

There was an ordinary, rather shabby wooden table in the center of Mal-binizar's secret chamber (a filthy basement under a disreputable tavern in the worst part of the Villains Quarter: Black mages not being welcome in more discriminating circles). He pulled back the frayed cuffs of his robe, laid his wand pointed toward the center of the city, then placed Bel-ama's wand so its tip was just touching the butt of his wand, with both of them in a carefully straight line.

"Um...is this trip necessary? I know you have issues, but isn't this rather extreme?" Ja-moke watched these goings-on uneasily around Mal-binizar's shoulder. He was getting a bit desperate as the Hour Of Doom approached, but had run out of ideas for how to prevent it.

Mal-binizar ignored him, and spent the next several minutes fussing and fidgeting until everything was just so. "Right," he grunted as he squared his narrow shoulders and straightened his tattered robe. His eyes burned with a feral gleam; he'd worked obsessively toward this day for half a century, enduring endless setbacks from his fellow mages, the city fathers, and even the Gods themselves. Despite their combined efforts, he now stood at his moment of triumph so long dreamt of. He was feeling his oats that morning, he was. So, of course, before destroying the world, introductions seemed in order.

"Now I'll show all you arrogant swine who laughed at me!" he threw back his head and yelled to the world. "It's payback time for all the insults and brickbats of the last *eight hundred* years by an unfeeling community, and especially..." he paused for breath, he did tend to run on, "...especially those unworthy cretins who presume to call themselves my fellow mages!" Mal-binizar did, indeed, have issues.

"Shaddap down dere!" came a crude grunt from above, accompanied by coarse laughter from the inn's patronage and loud thumps which shook a thick cloud of dust down on them.

"You are an ant!" Mal-binizar hurled back. "You are all less than ants under my feet."

"Harrr, if oim a ant, oil come down and bite yer donkey ears. Right lads?" There was another round of coarse laughter and more dust, accompanied by a chorus of, "Hee-haw! Hee-haw! Hee-haw!"

"Don't." Ja-moke laid a hand on Mal-binizar's arm as he was about to reach for his wand. "It's not worth the trouble."

"Right." Mal-binizar bit back his fury with an effort as his enormous donkey ears quivered in rage. The Old Ones *do* exact a price, and believe it or not, they have a sense of humor. The city was protected by its patron Gods, and their barrier spells inhibited magic enough so the dregs who frequented the inn above felt they could ridicule him with impunity.

"Hoy!" the innkeeper's voice came down through the rafters. "Last week yer called me a dog. So now oi'm a ant, eh?"

"Only because you lack the wit to be a dog!" Mal-binizar yelled, forgetting Ja-moke's good advice.

"Well what-say yer turn Lars 'ere into a cat? Oi could use a bit of pussy 'bout now!" There followed more laughter and the sound of fists, plus a lot more dust.

"You see what I put up with?" Mal-binizar turned to Ja-moke with tears in his eyes. "On top of everything else, they stole my ball of lint again last week!"

Ja-moke looked around in surprise. "They did! How on earth did they get it through the door?"

"I've never figured that out." But it kindled his rage again. "And where is my ball of lint, you swine?"

"Arf! Arf! Arf!"

"Wha? Now oi'm a swine, eh?"

"Oink! Oink! Oink!"

"Oi sold it t' the paper-makers t' pay yer back rent, is where it went. Yer Old Ones'll make yer collect another, which'll keep yers shut up fer a while, right lads?"

"Oink! Oink!" Stomp stomp. "Arf! Arf!"

"Dreadful," Ja-moke tisked. "Cretins, the lot of them." Then seizing on the opportunity, he added, "Say, are you *really* sure you want to use your spell on them? Putting them out of their misery is more than they deserve."

That put Mal-binizar in a bind.

"After all, anyone stupid enough to provoke a Black wizard deserves to live their miserable lives for as long as possible."

"Um..."

"Arf! Arf! Hee-haw! Hee-haw! Oink! Oink! Meow!" came a ribald chorus from above, plus more dust.

"You are ants!" Mal-binizar shrieked at the ceiling. "I'll make you pay a dear price for your fun, you dogs!" With that, he turned to the table, his mind made up, as Ja-moke silently cursed the louts in the inn above.

"And here we go," Mal-binizar hissed. He stood at the edge of the table, resting his fingers lightly on Bel-ama's wand and began chanting the vampire spell in its horrid Black Speech. Ja-moke stood by silently, watching the incantation in atavistic horror, feeling all goose-pimply, nervously wondering if this would hurt, saying one last good-by to the Goddess, thinking he had to pee. Mal-binizar finished the spell with a snarl of triumph, the linked wands flared, and both wizards involuntarily cowered as a blinding flash of *that-colored* light filled the room!

And then nothing.

"Mmmm, there seems to be a problem here," Ja-moke noted after a bit. They could still hear the street noises of a bustling city-state and the riot going on overhead, which appeared to have been joined by the city watch. And for that matter, Ja-moke was still alive, himself. Obviously Mal-binizar's Doomsday vampire spell misfired somehow.

"I...don't understand..." Mal-binizar's earlier swagger had evaporated. "The incantation is a simple one. And I got past the lock on Bel-ama's wand and...whoa! What have we here?"

The two wands still lay in a neat row, the tip of Bel-ama's wand just touching the base of his. But now a tiny *that-colored* figure lay sprawled on the table a few inches beyond the tip of his wand. It was a perfect man shape (except for being proportionally stockier like tiny humanoids always are) and he was dressed in a black T shirt, a black set of leathers and some assorted silver rings and chains. One of his tiny boots lay a short distance away, still laced up.

Then there was a click from Bel-ama's wand, and as they watched dumbfounded, a section of one side folded back like a tiny hatch, and a second *that-colored* figure wiggled his way out. This one was dressed in a purple kimono with a matching towel wrapped around his neck. His hair was wet and he was barefoot. Jumping down from the wand, he scurried over to the prostrate figure and knelt beside him anxiously.

The two wizards watched, befuddled, as the tiny figure felt for a pulse, then put his ear to the others chest. A moment of this, and he tried shaking the other, to no effect. He then leapt to his feet and turned to face them. "You...IDIOT! he yelled, setting their ears to throbbing. "LOOK what you've done!"

"Hoy!" the innkeeper's voice came down through the ceiling. "You tell 'im!"

"Watch out, 'el turn yers into a cat!"

"Meow! Meow! Arf! Arf!"

Mal-binizar was at a loss. "Um, what have I done?"

"He's dead!"

"Sorry..." Mal-binizar was a bit disoriented because he expected to be a God by now. This really wasn't working out as he planned.

"Idiot," the little man grumbled. "Utter damned mortal idiot." He paced back and forth for a bit, then stood looking at the inert body morosely.

"Um..." Mal-binizar studied the *that-colored* figure curiously. "...just what are you, anyway?" In all his centuries of mageing, he thought he had seen every arcane creature in the list, but this little chap was news to him.

"I'm a Pheauzee," the little man grunted absently.

"A...what?  What is a Pheauzee?  Are you a kind of Sprite, or Spirit Folk, or what?"

"Sprite HELL!  We're Supernatural Races, bub!"  The *that-colored* figure spun to face him menacingly.  "You know: Harpies, Furies, Pheauzees.  We're all part of the whole torment-of-mortal-kind thing."

"You, um, don't really look the part."  Tact was not Mal-binizar' long suit.

"Yeah?" the tiny *that-colored* figure sneered.  "You want to arm wrestle?"

"No!  ...uh, no, thank you."  Mal-binizar retreated hastily as the tiny figure's arm enlarged to where it was bigger than his.  The muscles had muscles.

Just then there was a faint POP! and a tiny round portal appeared on the tabletop.  A moment later, two more Pheauzees stepped through, carrying a stretcher between them.  These were dressed in identical neat white tunics, and a small white carpet bag lay on the stretcher.  The purple Pheauzee glanced nervously at them and quickly shrank his arm back to normal.  They dropped the stretcher, knelt by the inert figure, and began pulling tiny medical instruments out of the bag.

While they worked, Mal-binizar was able to collect his wits.  Obviously, whatever went wrong with his magnum opus of sorcery involved these two somehow.  Finally he got up the nerve to ask, "Um, I was wondering, just what do you two have to do in all this?  Do you, like, inhabit those wands?"  He tried to peer into the tiny hatch which was still open on Bel-ama's wand without seeming obvious.

"Well what the heck do you suppose makes a wand work, anyway?  Of course we inhabit them.  When you mortals orient a new wand, you make it a home for one of us."

"And you amplify spells in return?"

"It pays the bills."  The little man shrugged.

This was news.  Neither of them had ever considered the question of why wands did what they did.  Mal-binizar began to suspect he should have paid more attention in grade school science class.

"But what happened just now? I thought that spell would go through with no problem."

The tiny *that-colored* figure looked at him silently for a long moment, then muttered, "Utterly. Damned. Clueless. It's freakin' Arcane Powers 101, fools."

"I'm afraid you lost me."

"We can only take so much power," the little man said patiently. "Did you ever think of that? When we're young and just starting out in a new wand, we can't do very much. But as time goes along and our strength grows with practice, we can handle more spell energy. That's why your wand got to be so powerful after all these years."

"But..."

"But when you tried to pump the power of my wand through his, the multiplied charge fried him to a crisp." He directed a worried glance to the two attendants, one of whom turned to him and nodded sadly. They put their instruments back in the bag, then gently lifted the inert figure onto the stretcher, covering him with a tiny sheet.

"I'm sorry about your friend," Ja-moke said softly. "It was an accident."

"Actually, he was no friend of mine." The tiny figure was calmer now. "In fact, we hardly knew each other, him being a Black and me being a Purple, and all. Not that I have anything against Blacks, mind you! It's just, well, we don't frequent the same circles. Plus, we don't get to socialize much once we enter a wand."

"Because of the wizards lock!" Mal-binizar said, brightly.

The tiny figure put his hands on his hips and looked at him, shaking his head sadly. "Genius. Sheer genius. It's a wonder your species keeps going. Not that it's my problem any more!" He raised his arms and made a quick finger-snapping gesture; his purple kimono transformed into a hula print shirt and tan shorts. "I'm out of here!" he chortled, "'cause Doomsday Boy just unlocked my wand!"

"What? Wait! I own that wand now! I need you in there!" Mal-binizar cried.

"And you're welcome to it!" the *that-colored* man yelled cheerfully. "No way I'm going back in there with a head-case like you on the loose!" He made another finger-snapping gesture, and a pair of tiny suitcases appeared. "Besides, after 650 years, I rate a little vacation time!"

"But what about my wand?" Mal-binizar cried in anguish. It was the most important possession any wizard could have. Without it, he was helpless. "Can't you fix it?"

"Sorry." The little *that-colored* figure shrugged. "You overloaded your wand and burned out the Pheauzee. It's a deader...as I suspect you are!" he added hastily, for the room suddenly tingled with the arcane power of the outermost void. The two attendants looked at each other in alarm, scooped the stretcher up and hustled it through the portal. The Pheauzee from Bel-ama's wand followed quickly, but paused for a moment with one foot through the round nothingness. "Ciao, baby!" he called to them with a wave, then stepped through. The portal vanished.

The two wizards looked dumbfounded at the bare table and the two inert pieces of wood lying in a neat line, then at each other in dismay. The air was quivering with a deep, steady hum like a gigantic bell...the bell-tone of a connection between the outer void and their mortal plane. The Old Ones were coming. *All* of them.

Ja-moke shook off his bemusement and reached for his own wand, then he paused, and his hand dropped in defeat. What good would a 200 year old Green wand do against amassed ranks of the Old Ones? "Oh, well." He gave Mal-binizar a quirky little smile. "At least we learned something new today. It's always a good day when you learn something new."

Mal-binizar took small comfort in that, or that he'd been right about one thing at least: the Old Ones clearly did not care to see him exalted above them.

"I don't suppose it matters about Atlantis any more," Ja-moke added over the rising wind. "Once they get here without an evocation to contain them."

"Um...no." Mal-binizar the Black sighed. "I don't suppose."

\*\*\*\*\*

## "Interregnum"

Millions of years later...
...after the earth reformed, and life emerged anew...

# "Roadquest!"

## "Prologue"

And it came to pass that the Elfin kindred grew weary of the wicked ways of the world (for 'struth, all their jobs were exported to Singapore). Bitter was their lot when the feed mill closed, joining a long line of businesses which had shuttered their doors, leaving nought but a cavernous Wal-mart standing alone amid an asphalt sea of desolation. And they cried out in their despair, and gathered before their Ancient Seer to seek guidance and council, saying, "What we gonna do now?"

"Ain't nothin' we can do here," he cackled in senile glee. "This-here place is played out. We gotta find us the Promised Land." He gestured vaguely to the west and the vast Brown River in the distance. "There's a rich land right over yonder in the Bayou ripe for the takin'."

"Cool! Road trip!" they exclaimed in wonder, and stampeded from their ancestral lands to seek their new home in the Promised Land of the Bayou across the mighty Brown River.

But heavy were the hearts of the kindred when they came to the great river, for it was vast and treacherous. Worse, it was wet. And cold. And full of alligators. And they gathered before their Ancient Seer to seek answers and explanations, saying, "What now, smart ass? You expect us t' walk on water, or sumpthin'? It's wet an' cold, an' there's 'gators in there!"

"Ain't nothin' to it," he cackled in senile glee. "I'll just get them waters t' part, and we'll walk across."

"Eh...you sure about that?" they exclaimed in wonder.

"Hey, I ain't yo' Ancient Seer fer nuttin'!"

"Yeah, well, there is that," they exclaimed, doubtfully.

And he took himself down to the river and summoned the Elfin kindred to him, saying, "I'm gonna part this-here river, and you go marchin' right on across." He then stood upon the riverbank, raised his arms in the best Cecil B. DeMille fashion, and cried out, "Open Sesame!" The Elfin kindred, overwhelmed by this Technicolor spectacle, surged forth in joy, seeking the Promised Land in the Bayou.

The river did *not* part.    Dozens of them were drowned. Thwarted, the survivors pondered their next course of action, wondering wot th' *heck* went wrong.    And they gathered before their Ancient Seer to seek platitudes and excuses, saying, "Now what, dumb-ass?  Lookit all them people been drownded!"

"Ain't nothin' to fret over," he cackled in senile glee.    "We'll just use that-thar bridge."  He waved vaguely at the mighty bridge which was built over the river and its lowlands in the days when the world was in black and white.

"Well why th' hell didn't you think of that earlier?" they exclaimed in annoyance.

And there rose a great debate among the kindred.    Some counseled they use common sense for a change, and ford the river by boats, though this meant a lot of honest work to build those boats.    Others blindly believed in their Ancient Seer, and chose to follow him on the high path, though many feared the powerful wains which were known to rumble across the bridge at unpredictable times.

So it came to pass, also, that the Elfin kindred were sundered by this great philosophical schism.    Many—known ever after as the Low Elves—set off to a local Home Improvement center while others—known ever after as the High Elves—dared the windy passage over the mighty bridge.

And Lo!  As feared, an enormous freight wain did come as they crossed the bridge.  Many were swept away by the mighty wain never to be seen again, while many more were trampled, and some jumped (or were pushed, the tabloids claimed later) from the high bridge.  'Struth, it was quite a show.

Those Who Fell landed in the river near the Low Elves who were passing below in john boats and rubber inner tubes.  And did those Low Elves succor their estranged kindred in simple charity? Of course not, for they thought it hilarious, and poked ribald fun at them while most were drowned.    Most, but not all: for a few managed to cling to random logs or the Low Elves' john boats despite their kindred trying to drive them off, and thus were carried to the far shore.  And those who fell from height and survived were known ever after as the Middle Elves.

At last the surviving Elves were reunited on the far shore of the Brown River, and gazed in wonder at the land around them. It was a rich land, as prophesied: rich in insects, rich in snakes, rich in weeds and tangled undergrowth, and rich in water. Indeed, it was too rich, especially in water, as the mighty Brown River was bordered by boggy lowlands stretching for many a league. Despite their disappointment, they saw they had found their new home for it was uninhabited, because it was pretty near uninhabitable.

And their Ancient Seer looked upon this and made a mighty Prophecy: "That river'll come up every spring, bet your boots!" he cackled in senile glee. "We can't park down here, those levees will never hold!"

"Yeah, right," they exclaimed in contempt.

But for once he was right. The river came up as predicted and flooded the land for miles around, sweeping away the homes of the Elfin kindred who foolishly disregarded the warning, though in truth the Ancient Seer was as surprised as any of them. But even in their despair, they found comfort in the disaster, for the waters washed away a year's accumulation of trash along with their shabby tarpaper shacks. Undaunted, they rebuilt their homes and began accumulating new trash—only to have it happen again the next year. And the next. And the next. And the next...

At long last, running low on tarpaper, they heeded the wisdom of the Ancient Seer and made their homes on wheels so they might migrate when the waters rose. That problem solved, they turned their attention to other pressing issues: namely their sunburns, for 'struth the sun shone fiercely in these parts.

And great dissent grew among the kindred, for the Middle Elves had by some Darwinian miscarriage mostly become business owners and overseers, and now deemed themselves too good to associate with their lesser kin. They would lounge in the shade in their gated compounds during the heat of the day swatting flies and drinking Billy Beer while the Low Elves perforce labored in the fields and were horribly burnt. Their outcries were great, and the Middle Elves, fearful of their wrath, gave them cotton shirts and straw hats (on account at the company store) so they were no longer burnt except above their collars.

But as little as this gesture was, it was hardly enough to placate the rising tide of the Low Elves' anger. For now the Low Elves became angered and made many demands for improvement in their lives, notably pants to go with their new shirts. There was much hard feeling and estrangement between the Elves, guns and canned goods were stockpiled, and there was dark muttering about keeping "them" in their place, until a miracle happened which promised to reunite the kindred and change the course of Elfin kind forever.

For it also came to pass, in addition, that one of the Middle Elves sired a child by a Lower Elf waitress at the local diner. The newborn was named Uberbubba. The coming of Uberbubba was accompanied by rumors (from whence no one ever learned) of the birth of a Messiah who would bring great changes to their wretched lives. The Elfin kindred celebrated late into the night, got roaring drunk on bad moonshine, burnt down the City Hall, and generally proclaimed his coming in wonder, dubbing him the first of the Lower-Middle—or Redneck—Elves, and everyone was miserably hung over the next morning.

Little did they realize, then or later, how stupid listening to such rumors was.

§

## "The Long-Avoided Responsibility"

Years passed, and as the infant Uberbubba grew, he had many 'interesting' adventures (which were lost to mortal knowledge because his record was sealed by the juvenile court). He did all the things Lower-Middle Elf youngsters did in those days: dropped out of grade school; set random fires; 'liberated' mail boxes, cars, and anything else not nailed down; got a couple under-age Elf maidens in trouble (Lower Elves of course-one has standards); and developed an *unhealthy* interest in sheep. Somewhere along the way he blossomed into the full flower of (physical) adulthood; short and squat, with a beer gut and narrow piggy eyes which lit up when watching small animals suffer. And all the while he ignored the growing Legend of his miraculous birth as best he could, despite being constantly hounded about it by the expectant Elves.

"So when you gonna get about savin' us?" they demanded time and again.

"Yeah, well, I'm workin' on it," he'd reply, and would move along before the questioners realized he wasn't in fact saving them on the spot.

"Ain't he somethin'?" they'd say, admiringly. "Dang if I don't feel saved already."

"Speakin' of saved, I got me a jug of 'shine I been savin' since Tuesday fer a special occasion. Let's open 'er up."

So it was that as Uberbubba's Legend grew it wrought great change upon the Elves despite his evasions, as the rise in acute alcoholism showed. His supposed Prophecy had its effect upon him, as well. He learned to write his name, at least, from endlessly signing autographs, and ruined his liver with all the free drinks offered him. But while it affected him in many ways, none of them proved useful. He remained the same petty, unimaginative, lazy Uberbubba as always.

Eventually he became too hung over to follow the calling of a young hell-raiser, and settled into obscure mediocrity. He spent his days in his battered john boat out on the Brown River fishing for engine blocks, and because of that and his neighbors' dim-witted lack of imagination he came to be known as Uberbubba The Fisherman. It was a good living, by Lower-Middle Elf standards, for there was a steady demand for auto parts to repair their homes on wheels before the annual floods came. Small block Chevys were the most popular catch, of course, although Fords were useful and even Chryslers would do in a pinch. (Once he hooked an entire BMW, but the head gasket was blown so he regretfully threw it back, thus never finding the remains of Jimmy Hoffa in the trunk.)

If there was one fly in the ointment of his complacent life, it was his next door neighbor, Jimminy Cracker (of the Bayou Crackers), whose sole purpose in life, it seemed, was to bug him about the supposed Prophecy he was saddled with at a too-tender age which had grown into an article of faith among the Elves.

"When you gonna get to it, boy?" Jimminy would sit on the dock while Uberbubba was trying to fish, and kept up the same annoying monologue day after day while guzzling home brew. "You supposed to be this great Messiah what's gonna save us all.

People countin' on you, Lawd knows why." He paused for another swig of White Lightning from an old Mason jar. "Bout time you got off yer dead ass, don'tja think?"

Such talk always made Uberbubba uneasy, since thinking never was his long suit to begin with. "So who appointed you my conscience anyway, Jimminy Cracker?"

"Ain't nobody 'pointed me nothin'." Another swig of home brew. "I'm just a self-righteous ol' coot what figgers he can bug the hell out-a you on account of that-there Prophecy."

"Oh. That makes as much sense as anythin', I guess." Uberbubba made a point of turning his back, baited his hook with an empty oil can, and dipped it back in the Brown River. Maybe, just maybe, today was the day Jimminy Cracker would take the hint and shut the *fuck* up about that damned Prophecy.

"So? What's keepin' you? Don't you want t' improve yo'self none? You happy with this life, boy?"

No such luck. "I'm as happy as a tornado in a trailer park, thank you. Not that it matters t' *you*."

Actually, that wasn't quite true. As annoying as the Great Prophecy was, he couldn't help but wonder why he, of all people, was saddled with it. The mystery bugged him as he sat staring out across the Brown River in a funk. Supposedly there was a reason for the Prophecy, although he was darned if he could see it. He was stuck with some purpose he was supposed to serve, some mystery to solve which would save the Elves, although why he should bother was beyond him. But it got him no end of free drinks, so it must mean *something*.

"Save us from what, anyway?" he asked at last.

Jimminy Cracker spat his tobacce chaw and took another swig of White Lightning. "Danged if I know. Save us Elves from ourselfs, I guess."

"*That* would take a freakin' miracle."

"Wot th' hell you think a Messiah is for, huh?"

Good question. Uberbubba pondered that for some time, watching the Brown River with his thousand yard stare as it swept past, feeling the damp heat pressing on his back, ignoring the flies which kept buzzing around his head. No one ever quite put it that way before, and it evoked all his self-doubts and uncertainties over the Great Prophecy he was stuck with. *If* he was a Messiah like everyone said, and *if* he was supposed to save the Elves from themselves like everyone expected, and *if* it would require a freakin' miracle which it clearly would, then why was it *his* job to deliver? For that matter, he'd never performed a miracle before (aside from talking his way out of trouble with the law), and had no idea what to do. How does one perform a miracle, freakin' or otherwise, anyway? Uberbubba was beginning to suspect his world view wasn't nearly wide enough to cope with this mess. What to do? A huge blue-bottle fly was trying to crawl up his nose; time to act.

"All right," he said at last as he waved the fly away. "If I'm supposed to save us Elves, I best get to it. Then maybe you'll shut the *fuck* up an' quit mooching my White Lightning."

"Fat chance o' *that*, Miracle-boy!"

Whatever. Uberbubba hauled his john boat up on the levee and trundled over to his home parked nearby. His place was an ordinary single-wide with a screen porch on the side, done up in crude camouflage with spray cans and a plastic tarp stretched over the roof; typically Lower-Middle middle class. The suspension sagged and the floor boards creaked as he hauled himself through the narrow door. The inside was done in classic Early Redneck Elf bachelor: piled dishes, overflowing trash, sacks of aluminum cans, and ratty furnishings with the stuffing coming out the seams. He paused in the dinette, brushed the cobwebs aside, and looked around, wondering what to do next.

Well since he would be traveling, he decided to look his best. He dug through the dirty laundry for the cleanest set of skivvies he could find, added his favorite tattered old jeans and his XXL Nascar T-shirt, then paused to examine himself in the mirror. "Damn, boy. You one good lookin' sumbitch," he muttered as he slicked his scraggly hair down. He hadn't shaved in a week, but that was nothing unusual, so he let it pass. As a last minute thought, he packed a sandwich, some cookies, and a thermos of corn liquor in his old stamped tin Howdy Doody lunchbox before heading out again.

"You still got that piece of junk?" Jimminy demanded when he saw it. The thing was rusty and battered, the handle broke off long ago, and he'd replaced it with some baling wire and duct tape.

"Yeah. I've had it since the first grade, and it's precious to me."

"Like t' give you food poisoning. Ain't you never cleaned it in all this time?"

"Why? It'll just get dirty again tomorrow." That argument being unanswerable, Jimminy Cracker let it drop.

But time was a-wastin'. Uberbubba turned to plowing through the piled auto parts, old lawn furniture and assorted junk to dig his wheels out from behind the house. At least he'd travel in style, since his wagon was brand spankin' new.

Jimminy examined Uberbubba's wagon enviously when he hauled it out into the light. "Fishin' fer engine blocks been good, huh, boy?" he said as he admired the genuine wood slat side boards and the bright red enamel finish.

"Yep. Had me a run of small-block Chevys lately."

"Lawdy, a gen-U-wine Radio Flyer. You been on eBay again, huh? Some people got all the luck."

Uberbubba eyed Jimminy severely. "I *live* here. You call this luck?" He tossed his lunchbox in the back, climbed in, and swung the handle back and forth a few times to get the feel of it. He may have reached physical maturity, but *mental* was another matter. "I'm out'a here and off to find my destiny!"

About twenty minutes later Jimminy said, "You gotta pull that thing, you know. Don't go by itself."

"Oh." Uberbubba climbed out reluctantly, grabbed the handle, and set off down the road.

"So where you goin' boy?"

Uberbubba thought about it for a bit, then stopped, then turned around and went back to where Jimminy was watching in the distance. "Ah...I dunno."

"You want some good advice?"

"No."

"Go see Yokel, The Wise Hermit. He'll straighten your sorry ass out."

§

78

## "The Long And Winding Road"

Uberbubba had no idea where he was going at first, so he made good time. It wasn't long before he picked up the county highway and headed north, wondering all the while what adventures lay in store over the horizon. The day was miserably hot, as always, and the highway was a winding, narrow rut hemmed in by second growth timber and tall weeds which trapped the humid air. It wasn't long before his feet began to hurt, and he began sampling his thermos of corn liquor, just for the heat, of course. By time he'd gone a couple miles, he wasn't feeling the heat at all.

"Damn-fool way t' make a livin'," he grumbled for the umpteenth time as he trudged along. "How's a feller s'posed t' travel when he don't know what's what." He sampled his thermos again. "Dang, out of hooch, too. This bein' a Messiah is for the birds."

He plowed on through mid day, grumbling to himself and cursing his ill-luck at being The Chosen One without really caring where he was going, or why. The flies and 'skeeters and chiggers were lined up to take turns on him as he struggled along. His arm ached from hauling his wagon, his feet ached from the many stones and roots he stumbled over, and his head ached from a thermos of rotgut drunk on an empty stomach. It finally occurred to him that since he wasn't riding in his Little Red Wagon, he should have left it behind. The damned thing seemed to weigh a ton, and wrestling it through the ruts was an endless hassle.

"I get back, somebody's gonna get it good fer this stinkin' Prophecy," he grumbled. If this was how a Heroic Quest was supposed to go, he wanted none of it. He'd gone almost three miles already, and the midday heat and the burning sun mixed with the dust and insects left him so bothered and weary that he hardly cared where he was or where he was headed. He was so inattentive in fact that he walked right off the road where it split in two directions, and landed face first in the Brown River.

"Ain't this some shit?" he groused as he dragged himself out of the mud. "This figgers, don't it?"

He stood on the levee, dripping and muddy, trying to collect his thoughts, then gave up and got to work hauling his Little Red

Wagon back onto dry land. That took more effort than he was used to since it felt like it was full of water all of a sudden.

"What's *with* this damned thing?" he grunted as he strained to keep the wheels from sinking into the soft earthen levee. It took way too much effort, but he finally got it up on dry land, and only then noticed it was in fact full to the brim with muddy river water.

"Aw, fer the love of (*expletive, deleted*)!" He hauled on the side of the wagon and managed to tip it up by main force and pour the water out along with an enormous catfish, which gave him a resounding whack across the shins with its tail before flopping back into the river.

"Darn, there goes lunch." That was doubly unfortunate since his precious Howdy Doody lunchbox was drifting off on the current.

It was only then he noticed the signs tacked to rotting 4 x 4s stuck right at the split in the road. He missed them earlier since they were tattered, mold-encrusted and all but buried in the weeds despite their being twenty feet tall. He'd walked right under them without noticing, in fact.

## Green Acres Model Development
### Scenic River View Lots
### Better Homes For A Better Community

## FEMA Evacuation Center

Uberbubba studied the signs for some time, but since he could scarcely read, he couldn't make heads or tails of them. Still, the road split here, and he needed to either make a choice or keep going as he was. Since he really didn't want to land in the Brown River again, he chose randomly to turn right.

Another couple hundred yards along the overgrown trail brought him to a clearing perched on the levee itself. The place was bare and uninviting, with a row of cheap prefab huts in front of what was probably a meeting hall. The huts were weatherbeaten, with broken windows and doors hanging loose. The place was worn and decrepit, and looked to be long abandoned. In the center of the open lot stood a bare flagpole surrounded by a ring of whitewashed stones all but buried in weeds and trash. Next to that was a broken down sign reading:

## Rural Development Initiative Center
### Building A Better Community
### For A Better Tomorrow

As he wandered around aimlessly, someone came out of one of the huts at the end of the row lugging a plastic garbage sack nearly as large as himself. He was a dwarf Dwarf (that is, a runt even by Dwarf standards, no doubt picked on by all the schoolyard bullies) and seemed at first to be dull green, but when he came closer, the green turned out to be a layer of fungus, not surprising in this humidity. He was wearing the tattered, moldy remnants of a red-white-and-blue team jacket with an illegibly faded logo which read "Vista Volunteer".

"You're Yokel, The Wise Hermit!"

The green pygmy greeted him with an annoyed glare. "So astute are you. Know everything you do." With that, he dumped the garbage sack at Uberbubba's feet and shuffled back toward the hut.

"But...wait! You got t' help me!" Uberbubba scuttled after him. "Everyone in these parts says t' see Yokel, The Wise Hermit."

"Fools in these parts everyone is. My name a comma has not."

He kept on into the hut with Uberbubba trailing after him pleading all the while. "Look, I need your advice. I've got no idea where I am, or where I'm supposed to go, or what I'm supposed t' do when I get there, or why I should bother in the first place. I need some help here."

"More than help you need," Yokel said as he kept ducking past Uberbubba. "A life you should get." He ignored him after that, wandering back and forth in the hut to avoid him, complaining all the while in a muttered undertone. "I cannot help this one. The fool has no paperwork."

"HE WILL CREATE PAPERWORK IF YOU TEACH HIM TO WRITE," a rich, sonorous voice—with a British accent, fancy that—echoed through the hut, causing UberBubba to jump with surprise. But Yokel ignored it and muttered on.

"So perceptive is he. A great world traveler he thinks himself. What knows he of anything? A bumpkin he is."

"MAYBE HE CAN BE TAUGHT," the booming voice echoed again. "BUT IT WON'T BE EASY."

"Gave up a career in law did I. In Manhattan I could be." Yokel hobbled back and forth spewing out his mumbled rant. "But no, serve my country I chose." He paused to take a stiff hit on a bong he pulled from his hip pocket, then went back to pacing. "Foolish idealistic youth I was. Foolish! Look at me now."

"KARMA IS A BITCH SOMETIMES."

Yokel ignored it as well, and went on bewailing his sorry lot to the universe. "Too long stranded in this pest-hole have I been. Rotten is everything with heat and humidity." He scratched at his moldy arm absently. "For a hot bath my soul I would give."

"YOU *WERE* SUPPOSED TO TEACH THEM ABOUT INDOOR PLUMBING."

"Try I have, but good it did not. A moldy green hell this is. Sorry is my fate."

"Um..." UberBubba asked diffidently when Yokel paused at one point to take another hit on his bong. "Who is that voice, anyway? Where does it come from?"

Yokel spun on him, eyes large in surprise and alarm. "Hear it too you can?" he squeaked.

UberBubba nodded. Yokel looked at him in stunned silence for a long moment, then sagged in a chair. "Oh, thank heaven!" he groaned as he buried his head in his hands. "Barking mad I thought I'd gone!"

"THAT WOULDN'T BE SURPRISING, SEEING HOW LONG YOU'VE BEEN HERE."

"You will help me, won't you? I need you if I am to fulfill the Prophecy made when I was born."

Yokel stared at him in dismay. "The Prophecy you bear? Poor fool you are." He turned away and took another hit on his bong.

"IS THAT LINE OF BULL STILL CIRCULATING?"

"Can you help me?" Uberbubba pleaded. "I got this damned Prophecy all over me like a rash."

Yokel gave him a guilty look. "Reunite the kindred you must if your Prophecy you would be free of. To seek the High Elves is your quest."

"The High Elves? I thought they were swept away long ago."

"THEY WERE, TO THE BIG CITY."

"But what does it mean? Where is this Big City, and why should I go there?"

"Where the High Elves are the Big City is. Go there you must if your Prophecy you are to fulfill."

"Huh? Wot th' hell good would those sissies be?"

"Known as the 'haves' and 'have-nots' the divided kindred are. The 'haves' they are, possessing what you Low Elves have not."

"YES, STREET SMARTS, A SENSE OF STYLE, BASIC SOCIAL SKILLS, EVERYTHING THE LOW ELVES LACK."

"But...I'm a Lower-Middle Elf."

"HMMM, MAKE THAT 'DESPERATELY LACK'."

Yokel recoiled in alarm. "A Redneck Elf you are!"

That got Uberbubba riled. "Yeah, that's right. What about it?"

"Yet the Prophecy he bears," Yokel muttered in dismay. "A Redneck Elf. Screwed up royally this is. Cope I cannot." He hit his bong, hard. "This farce will be with us always."

"Look, I don't know what your problem is, but I need your help if I'm to dump this damned Prophecy. Are you gonna help, or just sit there and mouth off?"

"Huh?" Yokel stared at him vaguely. "Que pasa, dude. Wassup?"

"LOOKS LIKE YOU SCORED SOME GOOD SHIT, MY MAN."

Uberbubba struggled to contain his temper, wondering all the while where Yokel kept his stash. "Look," he said slowly. "I. Need. Your. Help. To. Get. Rid. Of. This. Stinkin'. Prophecy. Will. You. Help. Me?"

"Um..." Yokel stared at him, blinking in watery-eyed confusion. "Munchies I have. Got any Fritos, man?"

"Uh, no. Sorry. Look, what am I supposed t' do?"

"Only in...Big City the answer to...Prophecy you can find," Yokel mumbled. "Urgent is your quest...multiply like rabbits Redneck Elves are."

"Well, I guess so." Uberbubba could testify to that. "So what about it?" But Yokel wasn't paying attention, being preoccupied with another massive bong hit.

"SO GIVE HIM THE ANCIENT WISDOM, ALREADY."

"Hey...earth to Yokel...you still with us there?"

"Huh?" Yokel stared around the room vaguely, staggered by shock and dismay and too many hits on his bong. "*What*, man?"

"GIVE HIM THE ANCIENT WISDOM. HE'LL NEED IT IF HE IS TO MAKE IT IN THE BIG CITY."

"Oh...um...yeah..." Yokel dropped his bong and started rooting through a low bookshelf full of ancient textbooks, dog-eared Readers' Digests, and an unabridged encyclopedia. They were tattered and moldering from a leaky roof, and they crumpled in his hands as Yokel pawed them. Finally he gave up, scooped up an armload of moldy pulp, and threw it on the table. The load scattered and crumpled into a soggy mass of yellowed, vermin-gnawed garbage.

"Here-za...here's...see f' you'self..."

Only one tiny fragment remained legible:

"See Dick. See Jane."

Uberbubba studied the cryptic fragment for some time. "But...what does it mean?"

"Plain Eng...lish is is," Yokel mumbled. "Un'er...stand you not words...one syl...la...ble?"

"No, I don't. But if I gotta go to the Big City to ditch this damned Prophecy, then I'd better get hoofin'."

He headed for the entrance, fed up with the whole scene and craving Fritos all of a sudden. Yokel watched him go in confusion, them stumbled along after him. "Walk all' way to...B-Big City you plan? Foolish this is."

"BUT NOT SURPRISING."

Uberbubba halted and turned on him. "Okay, Mister Know-It-All, so what do you suggest?"

§

**"The Fellowship Of The Lost"**

They headed back to the main highway with Yokel riding in the wagon because he was too stoned to navigate. Another hour or so backtracking brought them to a turn Uberbubba missed earlier, which lead them by nightfall to the first sign of civilization he'd seen all day:

## GREYHOUND STATION

He looked askance at Yokel. "*This* is your bright idea?"

"A magic carpet you would prefer?" Yokel was grumpy since his bong ran dry. "Air Force One maybe you can borrow?"

"HEY, IT BEATS WALKING."

"Yeah, I guess it does." Uberbubba sighed and kept on trudging with Yokel grumbling in the wagon behind him as he made his way along the cracked asphalt. This was his first hint of what the Big City must be like, and it was depressing. The place had a tattered, run down look, with boarded up windows, random trash in the street and derelict cars here and there; rather too much like the Low Elves' town, only bigger and fancier. Somewhere along the row of gas stations, fast food joints and adult bookstores, he passed a ratty billboard:

Welcome to

### Riverdale

Pop ~~570~~ ~~486~~ 340

And Getting Better Every Day!

"Oh, look," he griped. "A sign to guide our way."

"Know where we are now. Slower our journey will become."

"THERE'S HOPELESS FOR US YET."

Uberbubba was dazzled and bemused by the bright lights along the main drag which lit up the Bayou night, especially the garish neon display next door to the Greyhound Station:

85

GIRLS! GIRLS! GIRLS!
Live shows!  Sister acts 3 times nightly!
Hottest Babes In Town!


"Hell," he griped as he plodded along.  "Maybe I should forget this damned Prophecy and just head over there."

"More than answers you will get there maybe, hmmm?"

"SOME OF WHICH IS INCURABLE."

Finally he pulled into the parking lot, where he dumped Yokel and made his way through the trash and oil stains to the cheap glass and aluminum main building.   The inside was done in linoleum flooring, plastic wall panels, faded travel posters in the windows and rows of hard plastic seats in front of a broken TV monitor.  The Station Agent was a fat Troll sitting behind a glass enclosure munching donuts and reading a grease stained girlie magazine.  "You want somethin', pal?" he greeted Uberbubba with ill-concealed contempt.

"Yeah.  I wanna go to the Big City."

The Station Agent sniffed and gave him a jaundiced look.  "Ain't too picky, are ya?"

"I must not be if I'm here.  D'you go there or not?"

"All right, Columbus, have it your way."  The Station Agent ran his Visa card and cranked a ticket for him.  "Good luck, lil' cowboy."

Uberbubba examined the receipt doubtfully.  "So when does this get here?"

"Oh-God-Hundred of course, like all of 'em.  Unless there's traffic, which'll make it at least Oh-Hell-Thirty.  Maybe you'll get lucky: the one what was due here yesterday might show up any time now."

"If you call that luck."

"Yeah?  Well screw you, and thank you fer goin' Greyhound."

§

"Your shit sorted out you have?" Yokel greeted him when he headed for the waiting room.

"You again?  You want a tip or somethin'?"

"That much class expect you have I do not.  Not every day a

86

Redneck Elf out into the world goes. With great amusement watch the gyrations I will."

"YES. THIS OUGHT TO BE ENTERTAINING."

"Suit yourself."

On his way to the waiting room, Uberbubba bumped into a blowsy, overweight peroxide blond in a straining miniskirt and blouse who teetered unsteadily on six inch spiked heels. "Hey sailor," she mumbled. "Lookin' fer a lil comp'ny?"

"Um...sorry. I'm a bit lost."

"Ain't we all, honey?"

One thing nobody *ever* accused Uberbubba of was being a prude, but *this* bimbo was strictly from Dogmeat City. And since he didn't want to risk catching something incurable, "Um, if you'll excuse me..." He sidled past her, turned for the waiting room, and all but ran into someone else. "Who th' hell are you?"

"Who? Me?" The stranger looked him over. "I'm Elvin."

If he was an Elf, he was a most *peculiar* one. The white pants suit, diamond-encrusted sunglasses, and the scarlet-sequined electric guitar they could see, but those mutton chop sideburns...

"Weird he is," Yokel muttered.

"HE *IS* WAY TOO HEFTY FOR A PANTS SUIT."

"Yeah, right," Uberbubba scoffed. "No Elf I know would dress like that."

The stranger looked him up and down, and wasn't impressed. "Never been to Lost Vegas, huh? I wowed 'em on stage there, twice nightly."

"No accounting for taste, there is."

"BUT WHAT ACCOUNTS FOR THE LACK OF IT?"

The mysterious woman stared at him vaguely. "You look familiar... You ain't really Elvin, are you? You gotta be an impersonator."

"No, I really am Elvin. My folks was from these parts, and I come back to find my roots in the Bayou."

"You're one of the lost High Elves!" Uberbubba exclaimed in wonder.

"Yeah, that's right. I got my start locally, but made the big time in Lost Vegas, built a whole new career there."

"It *is* you!" she gushed. "I got all your albums, all the 45s." She paused and stared bleary-eyed at him. "But...you don't look like him at all," she added, mournfully. "Elvin was young and handsome and sexy. You jus' gone t' pot, ain't you?"

"Thank you," Elvin kvetched. "Thankyouverymuch."

"So...who are you, anyway?" Uberbubba asked her.

"Huh? Oh. M'name's Dorothy. Call me Dotty."

"Appropriate that name seems."

"DISTURBINGLY SO."

"What? Are you a High Elf too?"

"Yeah." She focussed on Uberbubba with an effort. "I'm just a sweet, innocent girl from Kansas."

"You ain't nothin' but a hound dog," Elvin grumbled.

"Kansas, huh? I heard they got bad tornados there."

"Ain't that the truth! We got 'em somethin' awful. There was this big-ol' twister hit my Aunt's farm, blew the whole house clean away, an' landed me here." She paused in confusion and looked around. "Been here all these years an' still don' know where I am. What is this place?"

"You're in the Bayou."

"The *Bayou*!? Lawdy! I gotta get out-a here! My Aunt used t'tell me if I was a bad girl, I'd wind up in the Bayou!"

Elvin looked her over with a disdainful sneer. "Seems like you fit right in around these parts."

She flipped him off vaguely. "A girl gotta make a livin'."

"Indeed," a stranger commented. "Employment opportunities in this region are dismal at best, particularly among unskilled female labor. The current EEOC statistics show unemployment in that demographic segment at nearly twenty-seven point thirty-five percent..."

"Whatever," she grumbled.

Uberbubba looked him over suspiciously since he appeared out of nowhere. This stranger was average height, average weight, average age, average build, average looks...average everything, with no distinguishing features at all. He was the sort, in fact, who would fade into the wallpaper unless he spoke up. "So who th' hell are you, anyway?"

"I'm Stapledon. I can provide infodumps on background and technical stuff, off-site plot developments, history, and a lot of other things you would never know otherwise..."

"Whatever."

"Whaddaya mean by that cheap-ass remark?" Dotty shrilled at Elvin. "You think I'm easy, don't ya?"

"I ain't *that* lonesome tonight."

"You makin' me out some kind-a tramp or somethin'?"

"You got somethin' for everybody, looks like."

The Greyhound arrived as they argued, and Uberbubba tried to sidle discretely toward the door. "Where are you going do you think?" Yokel demanded. "Since wheels you have a ride you must share. Leave me in this sink hole you will not."

"ARE YOU SURE THIS IS A GOOD IDEA?"

"What? You headed for the Big City?" Elvin demanded. "Mind if I tag along?" He didn't wait for an answer.

"I've got nothing better to do," Stapledon commented. "I'll come along as well, since I might have occasion to offer infodumps to inform everyone about a particular situation..."

"Whatever."

"And I'm going too!" Dotty added. "Uh... Where's my little Tote?" She looked around frantically. "There you are!" She grabbed a small travel case resting against a nearby post and extended the handle. "Shame on you! I was looking all over for you! Naughty Tote!"

"Too long out here she has been."

"UTTERLY BARKING."

"Wait for me, Elvin!" She hurried after him as he retreated into the parking lot. "I'm coming to Lost Vegas with you!"

"My wish come true," he sighed.

"Need this do we, a shivering neurotic?"

"SHE'S GOOD FOR SHITS AND GIGGLES ANYWAY."

Dotty staggered uncertainly out into the parking lot with Tote squeaking "Yip! Yip! Yip!" along behind.

"Oil that squeaking wheel can you not?" Yokel complained. "Mad it will drive us all."

"THAT WOULD BE A SHORT TRIP."

The lot attendant was busily hitching Uberbubba's wagon to the Greyhound, and eyed their sorry mob suspiciously. "What? All-a you goin' on this run?"

Uberbubba glanced at the others, who seemed clearly determined to bum a ride. "I guess," he sighed.

"Well hey, you didn't say nothin' about no extras. You're gonna need a second Greyhound fer this bunch."

"Um..." Uberbubba turned to the others, who hemmed and hawed, studied the ground, perused the magazine rack, and too-obviously avoided his gaze. "...anyone wanna pitch in on the fare?" They hemmed and hawed, studied the ground, perused the magazine rack, and too-obviously avoided his gaze. Finally he turned to the attendant with a weary sigh. "Set 'er up."

The lot attendant brought out a second Greyhound, which took one look at them and whimpered pitifully as it was added to the hitch. "I hope you know you're messin' up our operation all up and down the Brown River," he grumbled. "Assigning extra equipment like this ties the schedules all up in knots."

"Yeah, right. This wasn't my idea to begin with."

"Well there you are." The lot attendant finished the double hitch. "Get on your way and t' hell with you. And thank you for traveling Greyhound."

Everyone piled on, which proved more complicated than one would think since Uberbubba's Little Red Wagon was a tight fit for him alone. He had to drive, so he got to sit in front. Elvin promptly squeezed in behind him. Dotty plopped on his lap, to his dismay, her legs dangling out the back, and clutched her little Tote tightly to her chest. That left Yokel no choice but to settle for a perch on Uberbubba's lap. "Get bright ideas you should not," he lectured him severely. "Straight I am."

"Darn. Green's my favorite color."

Stapledon was the last, and since there was no place for him to squeeze in, he perforce had to stand precariously balanced on the wooden side rails with both hands on Uberbubba's head to steady himself. "All aboard," he commented. "I'll be fine, thank you. Actually I've been in worse predicaments, particularly the time when we were battling the Imperial Storm Troopers..."

"WHATEVER."

"Ain't this some shit?" Uberbubba sighed as he surveyed the sorry mob as best he could from his cramped position. "We've become a gen-U-wine Fellowship."

"Sexist pig," Dotty muttered.

§

## "The Nein Riders"

But their hopes of an easy journey to the Big City were not to be, for a Little-Red-Wagon-load of five plus Tote was a bit much even for a double hitch of Greyhounds. Even after they picked up the Interstate, their progress was glacial at best as the Greyhounds panted and whined. "Are we there yet?" soon became their single most popular subject of discussion, followed closely by assorted bitching and grumbling.

"You mind gettin' yer hands off my head?" Uberbubba griped at Stapledon for the umpteenth time in the last hour. "My neck's gettin' sore."

"Oh, sure," Stapledon commented. "It's just like you to think of yourself. What if I lose my balance and fall out of this wagon? I could get hurt!"

"What hurt? We're goin' at a walking pace."

"Are we there yet?"

"I could easily get run over by a truck..." Another semi roared past, buffeting them with its slipstream and air horn. "...which would ruin my whole day..."

"Whatever!"

"Getting hot it is. A shower you need."

"I DON'T KNOW ABOUT YOU, BUT I'M DYING OF BOREDOM."

"Maybe we could take a break, huh?" Elvin suggested.

"Are we there yet?"

"I gotta go t' the little room," Dotty added.

"Yeah, yeah, all right." Uberbubba guided the two Greyhounds through the off ramp into a rest area, and they piled out. "Lordy!" Uberbubba stretched to get the kinks out of his back. "Gettin' there *ain't* half the fun."

"How much longer this trip gonna take?" Elvin asked.

"Too long!" He surveyed the scene around them: a crumbled asphalt plaza with several big rigs parked in the distance and some vending machines under an open awning. "They have anything t' drink here?" The one vending machine in working order offered Irish Coffee, Greek Ouzo, Saki, Peppermint Schnapps, Stolichnaya Vodka (with soda), and Billy Beer. "Hot Damn!" Uberbubba fed some quarters into the slot and pulled the beer handle. "Dammit! Empty!"

"Too bad," Elvin said.

Uberbubba pulled the handle for Vodka. "Still nothing." Same with the Saki and Schnapps. "Well spit! Don't they service these things?" He hit the return button, but instead of his quarters, a light lit up: DON'T DRINK AND DRIVE.

"You're screwed, dude."

"What a rip!"

There was a sudden rumble, and a caravan of bikers pulled in off the highway. "Ogres!" Uberbubba said, nervously. There were nine of them, dressed in black leather jackets, black jeans, black boots and spiked coal bucket helmets, all festooned with silver chains, skull-and-crossbone badges, and swastika arm bands. They were armed with knives, pistols, shotguns and assault rifles, and one carried a bazooka.

"They look like trouble," Elvin said.

"Yeah, but they're so *buff*," Dotty sighed.

They roared up to where they were standing and circled around them like sharks, throttles gunning in an endless round of deep, intimidating rumbles. Finally they ground to a halt, dismounted, and circled them ominously. Once they had the Fellowship cornered, one of them, obviously the leader since he was the biggest and most vicious-looking of them all, and was armed with a tactical nuclear missile, spoke.

"We're the Nein Riders," he growled. "You heard of us?"

"Um...Nine?" Uberbubba asked.

"Too bad." They hefted their weapons...

"Not Nine," Yokel said, urgently. "Nein."

"Nein?"

"Ja, Nein," the leader said.

"The Nine Riders?"

"NO, NOT NINE RIDERS, THE NEIN RIDERS!"

"Nein?"

"Ja!"

"I don't get it. *Nein* Riders?"

"Ja, not Nine, Nein!"

"Nine?"

"Nein! Not Nine, Nein!"

"Nine?"

("What time is it?" Dotty murmured.)

("Noon.")

"Noon?"

"Can't be that late. It's hardly past nine."

"What? Nine already?"

"Ja, nine fifteen."

"Nine Fifteen Riders?"

"NEIN! Nein! Nein! Nein! Not Nine Fifteen! Nein! Nein Riders!"

"Must be 'cause there's Nine of them," Elvin offered.

"Nein, not nine," Yokel said.

"Ja! Nein, not Nine! Nein of us!"

"Nein?"

"Ja! Nein!"

"Ah...come again?"

"We're the Nine...ah...Nein...Now you got me confused!"

Just then there came an evil roar, and a maxed-out black Harley pulled into the parking lot. The Ogre riding it was dressed in a County Ranger uniform which barely fit his huge and enormously muscular frame. The Harley ground to a halt as the Nein Riders watched in silence. The Ranger dismounted coolly, and walked toward them, his boots squeaking on the gravel. The two Greyhounds, who had been watching the confrontation with the bikers in amusement, shivered and whined as he passed.

"You lookin' fer trouble, *pig?*" the gang leader snarled.

The Ranger wasn't the least fazed by being outnumbered nein to one, or by their massive arsenal. He took off his sunglasses; his eyes glowed red. "You vill leave now," he rumbled.

The gang leader shoved an AK-47 in the Ranger's face. "You forgot t' say please! Surely yo' momma taught you t' say please and thank you!"

Faster than lightning, the Ranger snatched the AK-47 out of his hands and broke it in two. "*Don't* call me Shirley!" he growled as he tied the gun barrel in a knot.

The gang leader was stunned by his violent show of strength. "Ah...yeah, sure dude. Anything you say." The Nein Riders backed away cautiously, climbed on their hogs and peeled out of there in a cloud of dust.

"Zey vill be back." The Ranger turned to the Fellowship. "Come mit me iff you vant to live."

He headed abruptly for his Harley as Uberbubba and the others scurried to keep up. "Hey, it sure was lucky you came along when you did," Uberbubba said to him.

"I vas sent here to protect you, Connor."

"Connor? Who's Connor?"

The Ranger stopped and turned to him. "You are not zee leader of zee human resistance?"

"Uh...no..."

"Oh. Vell zen, to hell mit you!" And with that he mounted his black Harley and peeled out of there in a cloud of dust with a hearty, "Hi Ho Silver!"

"Ain't he somethin'?" Dotty gushed.

"Somethin'," Uberbubba grumbled. "Let's get a move-on before those nine retards come back."

"Nein retards they are."

"*Don't* start that again!"

§
## "The Land Beyond The Map"

They eventually pulled into another Greyhound station at a quarter past Oh-God-hundred. Getting untangled and out of the Little Red Wagon took some doing; they were almost as stiff and sore as the two Greyhounds. The lot attendant took charge of those, and gave Uberbubba a venomous look as he led them to the kennel. The Fellowship, in turn, limped and straggled into the waiting room to sort themselves out.

"Lawdy," Uberbubba groaned. "What a miserable journey."

"Arrived at our destination at least we have," Yokel said. "Better than the Titanic, hmmm?"

"I'm not so sure about that."

"I'M GLAD I'M JUST A VOICE-OVER, SEEING HOW YOU ALL FEEL."

"Um...that is if we *have* arrived?" Uberbubba looked around the dingy waiting room; there were assorted Orcs, a couple Trolls and an elderly Goblin sitting on the plastic seats, but no signs. "How do we know this is the right place?"

"Ask someone you should."

Uberbubba gave Yokel a jaundiced look. "Ask directions? I thought you were straight."

"For you straight enough lil cowboy."

"THERE'S NO CHOICE. YOU'LL JUST HAVE TO GRIN AND BEAR IT."

"I guess." Uberbubba headed to the ticket counter where the station agent, an enormous, surly Ogre, sat reading a comic book. True to their reputation as sulking prima donnas, the brute ignored him as he stood in front of the window. "Um, excuse me..." he said at last. The Ogre was cool. His only reaction was to shift eyes to lock on him. "Can you tell me if this is the Big City, home of the High Elves?"

The Ogre reared up abruptly, towering over him in a thunderous rage. "You better watch your mouth, pal!" he roared, shaking his massive fists.

"Sorry!" Uberbubba backed away cautiously. The Ogre tore the ticket window frame loose and sent it hurling after him with a string of bellowed curses and threats. Uberbubba ducked the missile, and retreated back to the others with the curses burning his ears. "Any more bright ideas?" he demanded of Yokel.

"Uncooperative he is. Like High Elves he does not."

"NO SHIT, SHERLOCK."

"How about somethin' useful, huh?"

"There ought'a be a sign on the buildin'" Elvin suggested. "Or maybe we can ask someone on the street."

"I'm almost afraid to."

95

It was dawn.   The Greyhound station was in a run-down industrial district.   The morning light shimmered on dreary store fronts and dead neon signs dotting the landscape.   Several working types gathered around a parking lot barista hut under a sign reading, 'Alice's Restaurant', not far from the railroad tracks, while rusty old cars and pickup trucks crawled past bumper to bumper. The sidewalks were already crowded with the morning rush.   Orcs, Dwarves, and Goblins were everywhere, along with the odd Zombie, and the occasional busload of clueless human tourists who must have thought this was some sort of adventure ride.

"Only one of two places can this be," Yokel said, doubtfully. "Hiroshima, or the Big City."

"I'D PREFER HIROSHIMA, THANK YOU."

Stricken with doubt, they searched the area for some sign— finally coming across one a short distance away.   It was a bright red STOP sign once, but now it was faded by time and the elements to a sickly pink SLOW DOWN.   UberBubba gave a sigh of heartfelt relief.   "It's in color, so this can't be Hiroshima."

"DAMN."

"Well, it seems we're here, so let's get to it and find these High Elves."   Uberbubba flagged down the first Goblin, dressed in a plastic hard hat and work boots, who passed by.   "Hey pal, d'you know where we can find the High Elves?"

"Shit," the Goblin muttered.   "Just my luck to run into a bunch of weird-os."

"So what's with th' wise crack?   I'm lookin' fer th' High Elves, is all.   You got a problem wit' that?"

The Goblin backed away.   "Hey, I got nothin' against High Elves!"

"This ain't promising," Uberbubba griped as the Goblin scuttled away into the crowd.

"Now what?" Elvin asked.

"If at first you don't succeed, try, try again."

"The definition of insanity that is."

Uberbubba's next attempt was an Orc carrying a briefcase and dressed in a three piece suit and tie.   "Excuse me, neighbor.   Do you know where we can find the High Elves?"

The Orc looked him over suspiciously. "There are High Elves moving into this neighborhood?"

"Um...I dunno."

"I should hope not! We're trying to maintain a decent community. There's no low income housing in *this* area, *especially* for High Elves. It's against the zoning ordinances."

"Hey, I don't know from zoning ordinances; I'm just tryin' t' find 'em."

"Why? What would you want with *them*? You aren't one of *them*, are you?"

"Um, no. I'm a Lower-Middle Elf."

"A Redneck Elf!" The Orc was appalled. "As if *they* weren't bad enough!" He pushed past them and hurried on down the street muttering, "The whole damned city's gone to pot!"

"Seems they don't care much fer High Elves 'round here," Dotty said.

"But they do know of them," Stapledon commented. "To loathe them is to know them, so this must be the right place. We can surmise from the public reaction that the High Elves are unpopular and unwelcome in polite circles." He gestured down the street toward a broad lowland with squat tenements rising out of a dismal smog. "Such ill-favored minorities are usually confined to the ghetto in the least desirable part of town by socio-economic disadvantage...

"Whatever."

§

## "Close Encounters Of A *Disturbing* Kind"

There was nothing for it, so they set off down the street. The foot traffic soon vanished as the neighborhood deteriorated and the pavement sloped down hill, and before long they were alone, enveloped in the dense brown smog. They groped blindly down the crumpled sidewalk, tripping over uneven slabs and bumping into roadside signs. The smog was a choking miasma which stung their eyes and had them all wheezing. There was no sign of life other than dead weeds, and the air around them held a vague unnameable menace which made them all on edge.

"Creepy place," Yokel grumbled.

"Yeah," Dotty murmured. "They're out there, ain't they?"

"Almost better was the Bayou."

"Where can they be?"

An ominous booming rumble came out of the mists. "What? What's that sound? *A-are those war drums!?*"

"My Walkman. Sorry." The drumming stopped abruptly.

"D'you see anything?" Uberbubba whispered as he peered through the gloom trying to spot some sign of the High Elves.

"Well, I see you," Elvin said.

"And the street I see as well," Yokel added.

"Where's my little Tote? Oh, there you are!"

"Brilliant. So do you people *hear* anything?" Uberbubba searched the gloom nervously. *They* could be out there anywhere, watching, waiting...

"Yip! Yip! Yip!"

"Hear that unoiled wheel I do."

"I can hear your voice, and our collective footsteps, but this thick smog will tend to muffle ambient sounds..."

"Whatever."

"Fer cryin' out loud, people! D'any of you *see* anyone?"

"Testy, ain't he? I see Yokel and Elvin..."

"You I see not clearly..."

"And Dotty of course..."

"BUT NOT ME, SINCE I'M JUST A VOICE-OVER."

"I can't see Stapledon...

"I see England, I see France..."

"...oh, there you are..."

Uberbubba sighed in frustration. "Do any of you see, hear, feel, smell or taste anything or anyone other than us and this street we're on?"

"No, nothing. Why d'you ask?"

They emerged from the smog just then, and came up short at the sight of a horrid, utterly desolate landscape. Ahead of them was a derelict structure surrounded by mounded rubble and crumbled asphalt, with rusted cars and rotted furniture half-buried by blown dust and scattered trash. The windows were grime-encrusted and cracked, many of them boarded up. A couple mangled, rusty shopping carts lay on their side near by, and a feral dog growled at them and retreated.   UberBubba looked on in dismay, for he had never seen anything so hideous, so shocking, so depressing, so...so...so...utterly post-apocalyptic in his life. "Lordy!" he gasped.  "A thrift store!"

"Found your High Elves you have," Yokel muttered.

It was even worse than they feared, for the strip mall contained a check cashing place, a food bank, a store front church and a Senior Citizens center, with the brightly glowing glass and brick edifice of a Bank Of America branch looming over all like the ghastly temple of an insane God.

"Screw this!" Uberbubba cried.  "Th' High Elves can rot fer all I care.  I'm out-a here and back t' the Bayou!"

"Wisdom you show at last," Yokel said, fervently.

"DAMN STRAIGHT!"

They spun on their heels as one...

...to find a solid wall of High Elves across the road behind them.  Before any of them could cringe, the mob surged forward, grabbed them up on the fly, and hustled them down the street with a blood roar.  The High Elves were wild and excited, dressed in a motley array of do-rags and piercings and speedos and muscle shirts and Rebox and bomber jackets and jogging suits and sports Ts, and they were thrilled at their capture, shouting and capering and high-fiving each other.

"I thought they was supposed t' have a sense of style!" Uberbubba cried as they were carried along.

"HEY, I JUST READ THE LINES.  TAKE IT UP WITH THE AUTHOR."

The mob surged down the street like a flood, washing up at last in front of a run down tenement building.  Sitting on the wall in front were two enormous High Elves, identical twins from the look of them, short and squat and as round as two eggs.  They had broad frog faces, squinty eyes, and were bizarrely dressed in identical sailor suits, beanie caps and old school ties.  The mob hustled them up before the two and gathered around, hemming them in so they couldn't escape.  The frenzied roar of the crowd settled down into a dull rumble, and the two seated on the wall looked them over.

"Hi. We're the twins..." one said at last.

"...eldest sons of YoMamma..."

"...bringers of fear and destruction..."

"...harbingers of doom and despair..."

"...scourge of YoMamma's wrath..."

"...otherwise known as the Terrible Twos!"

"We're Leroy-Billy-Bob..."

"...and Billy-Bob-Leroy."

"Don't you *ever* call Leroy-Billy-Bob Billy-Bob-Leroy..."

"...or Billy-Bob-Leroy Leroy-Billy-Bob..."

(both) "Or we'll have to hurt you!"

"Um, sure, anything you say," Uberbubba said, doubtfully. "But which of you is which?"

The one on the left looked confused and turned to his brother. "Which one am I?" That brought on more bewildered expressions followed by a hasty conference. "We'll get back to you on that," they said at last.

"So...um...who are you?" the one on the right asked.

"We're from the Bayou. I'm stuck with that damned Prophecy."

"The Prophecy, huh? Poor bast'id. I *almost* feel sorry for ya."

"And you're from the Bayou? You're a Low Elf, ain'tja?"

"Well, a Lower-Middle Elf, actually."

"A Redneck Elf!" the one on the left gasped. "They let just *anyone* in here, don't they?"

"Well now, he can't help bein' what he is," the one on the right said, somberly. "Cut him some slack, eh? He might be potty trained, after all."

"Yeah, but..."

"Who knows? Maybe he can be taught t' read, or perhaps some useful trade. He might even join a union."

"Such good luck you will need," Yokel muttered.

The one on the right mused at Uberbubba for a moment. "So, why are you here, anyway?"

"We're here to see Dick."

A distinct chill descended over the High Elf mob, who fell silent. "Um...well, that sounds like a personal problem to me," the one on the left giggled.

"Yeah," the one on the right looked Elvin over with obvious distaste. "Don't have any of *that* in this neighborhood. You'll likely do better t' look uptown."

"Thanks. Um...which way is uptown?"

"Buckeroo, it's *all* uptown from here!"

"So how do we get there?"

Stapledon gestured to a tattered bus stop sign next to the street whose asphalt had long crumbled away, revealing the bricks laid back in the 30s. "The stop's right there, and the bus will be along any minute," he commented. "The High Elves are deeply offended by what they perceive as a gay proposition."

"What? Gay...?"

"If we make an obvious show of leaving the area, we will forestall a potential riot..."

"Whatever!"

"Yeah, what he said...I guess..."

"...noisy sumbuck..."

"...here comes the Yellow Line bus now..."

"...be on it..."

"...or under it."

§

## "The Mines Of More Excess"

They clambered onto the rickety Yellow Line bus and, needless to say, Uberbubba wound up paying all the fares. "Damn! We were lucky t' get out-a that one!" he sighed as they vanished into the smog.

"Open mouth, insert foot. Works every time," Elvin grumbled.

"So what do we do now? How can I reunite the kindred if th' High Elves done run us out-a town?"

Yokel gave him an annoyed glare. "Expect me to solve all your problems do you?"

"You're the brains of this outfit," Elvin said, pointedly.

"WE ARE IN BIG DOO-DOO."

"Well it's nice t' know you care!"

"Um, gee, I didn't know we cared," Dotty said.

The bus crawled up out of the smog-laden valley headed in the opposite direction from the Greyhound station. The neighborhood

101

improved steadily as they rode, with more traffic and fewer potholes. Before long the passing scene looked almost habitable, but it was a fleeting comfort. The further they went, the taller and more grandiose, and more ominous, the skyline became.

"Jeez, will ya' look at them buildings?" Dotty mumbled as they stared up at the glass and steel skyscrapers whose ground floors were lined with coffee bars, tanning salons and book stores. Their unease grew with each passing yellow cab, and the *disturbing* sight of a health club. Those warnings faded as they went further, to be replaced by faceless monoliths of fake granite and plate glass. Their unease grew, but what really alarmed them was their first sight of a stretch limo.

"It's the Corporate Ghetto!" Uberbubba said in dismay. "Like things weren't bad enough already!"

"Indeed," Stapledon commented. "We've entered Beamer Country, the Gated Community, home of the Upper Crust, Easy Street, the Miracle Mile, the Golden Rule, the Land Of Milk And Honey..."

"What*ever!*"

"*Now* look what you got us into!" Elvin complained. "We fer damn-sure don't fit in around here."

"*I'm* not drivin' the damned bus!"

"What are we goin' t' *do?*" Dotty whimpered in panic.

"Don't worry," Uberbubba assured her. "We'll just sit tight until we leave the area."

"Okay, everyone out. End of the line," the driver yelled as the bus ground to a halt.

"For that bright idea, so much," Yokel said in resignation.

"BEST LAID PLANS OF MICE AND REDNECK ELVES, I GUESS."

There was nothing for it, so they climbed off the bus and huddled on the sidewalk, gaping in dismay at the skyscrapers towering around them. "They'll bust us fer vagrants fer darn sure," Elvin kvetched as passers-by gave them fishy, vaguely hostile looks. "We'll be makin' gravel fer th' next twenty years."

"Everyone keep moving and act natural," Uberbubba said as he started down the sidewalk at a careful stroll.

"Suspicious that will make them especially," Yokel complained as he waddled after him. "The Bayou this is not. No place for acting natural this is."

"NOT WHAT *YOU* CALL ACTING NATURAL, ANYWAY."

"So what? We supposed t' do unnatural acts?" Dotty asked.

"On what you are into that depends."

The traffic made an endless din as limos and delivery trucks crawled past. At one point they passed a group of Orcs wearing Italian three piece suits and pink shirts, who eyed them coldly as they flowed around them as far away as the sidewalk allowed. "Lawyers!" Uberbubba gasped. There were more hostile looks from people wearing fine wool suits and mink coats—on a hot summer's day. Even bike messengers in tan shorts flashed them the finger and splattered them with water from a running fire hydrant as they wove in and out.

The street seemed to stretch on forever with an endless procession of enormous office buildings. The one they were passing stretched the entire block, and must have been fifty stories if it was an inch. "How do they drive them away when the floods come?" Uberbubba wondered.

"Floods they have not here."

"Rich sonsabitches got all the goodies, don't they?"

Just then they passed a newsstand. A headline on a stack of newspapers caught his attention:

RARE 1950s ARTIFACT TO BE AUCTIONED

Below that was a grainy photo of a battered tin box with a familiar printed image on its front and a familiar handle...

"Hey! My lunchbox!" It was indeed: unmistakably *his* Howdy Doody lunchbox complete with the baling-wire-and-duct-tape handle, only a lot cleaner and somewhat rustier after evidently soaking for days in the Brown River. "How'd they get ahold of that?" He grabbed a paper off the stack and poured over it avidly. After a bit, he turned sheepishly to the others. "Could...ah...someone read this to me?" Elvin gave him a derisive snort, took the paper and began reading:

*'A rare artifact from the 1950s, a cultural icon of early television, will go on auction today. This ancient lithographed sheet metal children's lunchbox is described by Socio-Anthropologists as being "A truly rare find in its unaltered original"...'*

"Hey, them's a lot'a big words."

*'...Despite being in poor condition due to long neglect, "a crime against history!" one observer complained, this discovery is drawing world-wide attention. "Most of the boxes you see today are either forgeries or have, tragically, been restored by well-meaning collectors ignorant of the consequences of their actions," one Sociologist explained...'*

"Ignorant? Who's ignorant?!"

*'..."The state of this find is unique, just as most of them must have looked after a school year." Despite being rated in 'crappy' condition by auction authorities, the bidding, to be held in a private invitation-only auction, is expected to be fierce...'*

"Hey!" the news stand proprietor shouted. "You gonna buy that paper, or do I call a cop?"

"Yeah, yeah, all right." Uberbubba dig in his pockets. "Um...I got no change." He turned to the others, who hemmed and hawed, studied the ground, perused the magazine rack, and too-obviously avoided his gaze. "Anybody got a quarter?"

"Well?" The news stand proprietor was a large Orc who clearly didn't have much patience with Elves.

"...workin' on it...guys?" The others hemmed and hawed, studied the ground, perused the magazine rack, and too-obviously avoided his gaze.

"You damned Elves think your sumpthin' special, don'tja? Well I'm as mad as hell, and I ain't gonna take it no more!"

"Sorry." Uberbubba folded the paper and tried to put it back.

"Like hell!  You pay up or I'll call a cop!"

"Um..."  One of the few things Uberbubba had going for him was his well-tuned instinct for talking his way out of trouble. Inspiration came galloping to the rescue.  "Hey, I understand how you feel.  You're completely right, an' I hate t' put you t' all that bother.  T' make it up t' you, you tell me where the police station is, an' I'll go right down an' turn myself in fer ya."

§

## "Door Number One..."

The nearest precinct station was six blocks away.  Uberbubba arrived with the newspaper folded under his arm and the rest of them straggling behind.  "All right!" he said with evident relish. "Now we're gonna get some action on findin' my precious lunchbox!"

"Uh...you ain't *really* gonna turn yourself in, are you?" Dotty asked.

"Hey, I'm not nearly as dumb as I look."

"YOU COULDN'T BE."

"Damn straight!"

"Gee, you fooled me."

"Fleeing for our lives we are supposed to be," Yokel complained.  "But charge into trouble now you will?"

"And what about your Prophecy?" Elvin asked.   "Ain't you supposed to be on a quest t' save the Elves or sumpthin?"

"T'hell with that!"  Uberbubba headed eagerly up the steps.  "I got more important things t' do."

The police station seemed deserted except for a bulky Dwarf with sergeant's stripes sitting behind the precinct desk.  He was leaned back in his chair, feet up, working a crossword puzzle, and ignored them as they halted in front of the desk.

"A three word phrase for a means to recover property," the sergeant announced without looking up.  "Twelve letters."

"Um...Lost And Found?"

"Right."  He scribbled in his booklet.

They stood uncertainly before the precinct desk for some time while the sergeant ignored them and worked his crossword puzzle. Finally Uberbubba spoke up.  "Um...excuse me..."

"A word meaning a philosophy of preserving old buildings. Twenty-eight letters."

"...Lost And Found?"

The sergeant paused and gave him an annoyed look. "That ain't twenty-eight letters."

"Uh...no, I want to report a Lost And Found item."

The sergeant sighed, laid his puzzle book aside, and swung his feet off the desk. The next several minutes passed in silence as they stared at each other. "Well?" he said at last.

"I want to report a Lost And Found item."

"You said that already. So what is it?"

"Oh." Uberbubba held out the newspaper photo. "That's my Howdy Doody lunchbox. I lost it, and it's gonna be auctioned off. It's precious t' me."

"So's my mother's virginity."

"But...it's mine! I lost it in a traffic accident, and I want it back. You gotta help me."

The sergeant was unimpressed. "You got a receipt for it?"

"Receipt? For a lost item?"

"No? How about an insurance claim?"

"Um...it wasn't insured."

"Stupid. How about the accident report?"

"I didn't file one."

The sergeant's eyes narrowed. "You didn't? Ya know ya gotta file an accident report. That's the law."

"Sorry. I didn't think I'd ever see it again, so I didn't bother."

The sergeant frowned. "If you came in here wit'out any documentation, that's filin' a frivolous claim as well." He opened a drawer and produced a pair of handcuffs. "The fines are gonna cost you somethin' awful."

"But I didn't know about this till I seen it in the paper! I don't have anythin' t' prove it's mine."

The sergeant scowled. "Well that-there is filin' a false claim. You can't claim somethin' unless you can prove it's yours." He produced a set of leg irons to go with the handcuffs. "Now you talked your way up to a felony."

"*What felony?* I didn't know I'd need a receipt!"

106

"Ignorance of the law is no excuse. You should'a thought of it 'fore you came traipsing in here all complainin' and makin' paperwork fer us."

"That's stuck on you," Elvin said.

The sergeant lumbered to his feet and added a wicked-looking truncheon to his collection. "You in a heap o' trouble, boy..."

"Happened out of this jurisdiction the accident did," Yokel said suddenly. "Filed with local authorities it was."

"Oh." The sergeant shrugged and settled in his chair again. "Then you'll have t' take it up with them." He put his feet up and went back to his crossword puzzle.

"But the cops down in the Bayou wouldn't have juris..."

Yokel yanked Uberbubba's sleeve hard enough to knock him off balance. "Busy the nice officer fighting crime is," he said as he dragged Uberbubba toward the door. "Bother him with trivial complaints you should not."

"But...my lunchbox...it's right there in the paper..."

"Weather report also is in the paper. Bother police with that you would too?" Yokel dragged him, protesting feebly, out into the street. "Remember this you should. Why save your sorry ass by lying I must is beyond me."

"I'M CONFUSED OVER THAT ONE AS WELL."

"But...my precious...my lunchbox..."

"If more important than your quest it is, then find it yourself you must. Police will help you not."

"So what'll you do now?" Dotty asked.

§

### "Door Number Two..."

"Ain't we supposed t' be savin' the Elves or sumpthin'?" Elvin grumbled for the umpteenth time. "What good's it gonna do t' see the newspaper? You gonna put an ad in or what?"

"T' hell with th' Elves! I want my lunchbox back! It's precious to me."

"But how they gonna help?" Dotty asked.

"They must know where this auction is. They can tell me where t' go."

"Hell, *I* can do that," Elvin said.

"But trust them can you?" Yokel asked.

"Well..." Uberbubba paused to thumb through the paper again. "It looks okay t' me."

"If ya don' consider all them girly photos," Elvin said.

"Or the headlines screaming about space aliens," Yokel added.

"OR THREE PAGES OF ESCORT ADS IN THE BACK."

"Gee...Was Hitler really a lesbian?" Dotty asked as she peered over Uberbubba's shoulder.

"Yep. Don' see what your problem is." Uberbubba folded the paper and started walking again.

"A fool such as I," Elvin sighed as they followed.

A few blocks further brought them to the largest, grandest building they'd seen yet; a towering skyscraper with an imposing staircase leading up to broad doors set between stone columns. An elderly Orc in a deep maroon uniform acted as the doorman.

"Jeez, some digs, huh?" Dotty said as they climbed the stairs.

"I wouldn't mind collecting the rent on this dump," Elvin replied.

"Good day, lady and gentlemen." The doorman bowed politely as they approached, and flashed them an ingratiating smile. "How may I be of service to you?"

"He got all kind'a swave and de-boner, don't he?" Dotty mumbled.

"We're looking fer a business at this place," Uberbubba said.

"Certainly, sir!" The doorman opened the doors with a sweeping gesture. "You will find the directory on your left."

The lobby was appropriately huge: lined with marble, two stories high with a row of elevators in back. A bank of metal detectors guarded the entrance. The color scheme was monotonous gray, it was studded with fake marble columns, and its only decor was a planter partially surrounding a shallow pool full of colorful koi fish.

Uberbubba came up short at the sight. "Whoa! Dinner!" One fish looked askance at him, then flipped a face full of water on him as it swam away.

"Barstid!" Uberbubba swore as he jumped into the pool and waded after the fish. "I'll have you with ketchup!"

"Ketchup on fish?" Yokel shook his head in despair.

"NOT THAT WAY. YOUR OTHER LEFT."

"Oh." Uberbubba waded back and sloshed his way across the lobby to the directory, which covered half the wall. They spent the next several minutes going over the endless list of names.

"I don't see 'em," Uberbubba said at last.

"Listed they are not," Yokel told him.

"NOT THAT HE COULD READ THE NAME ANYWAY."

"Well then, we'll have t' ask someone." Uberbubba looked around, then headed back to the main entrance.

"The strain is getting to him," Elvin muttered. "He's starting to make sense."

"Good day, lady and gentlemen." The doorman bowed politely as they approached again, and flashed them his ingratiating smile. "How may I be of service to you?"

"Where is the Daily Plant-It?"

The doorman's swave and de-boner vanished. "What? *That* bunch?" He gave them a disgusted look, and pointed to an obscure door in a back corner of the lobby, one they mistook for a janitor's closet. "They're over there, if you *must* know," he ground out. "Go on, get out'a here. I don't want any trouble out'a the lot of ya."

The door they were directed to was an old fashioned dark-stained wood panel type with frosted glass in the upper half. Printed on the glass in peel-and-stick letters was:

## The Daily Plant-it
### News The Others Won't Bother To Print

"This must be the place," Uberbubba said. The busy sounds of telephones ringing and typewriters going full-tilt came to them from behind the glass.

"Open the door the next step is," Yokel said, pointedly.

"DON'T ENCOURAGE HIM."

The interior was a shock compared to the opulent lobby. The room was small and crowded with battered old furniture. It had cheap plaster walls, a drop ceiling with hanging strip lights and two wood framed windows open in the back. There were a few cluttered desks, some battered file cabinets, a coat hook in one corner, and a couple brass spittoons. There were file folders and newspapers piled everywhere, and the place had a weary, worn look to it. It took them a moment to realize the whole scene was in black and white.

A bulky Troll in a cheap suit with a fedora tilted back on his head sat at an old wooden desk pecking away on an antique Underwood. A cigarette smoldered in a filthy ash tray full of butts by his elbow, and a dirty coffee cup left rings on the desk calendar. He looked up when they entered, then hit the STOP button on a reel-to-reel tape recorder, killing the office sounds. "Hi, I'm Mark Bent, mild-mannered reporter for the Daily Plant-it. You got a scoop, we got the liter box!"

Uberbubba unfolded the paper and threw it down in front of him. "That's my lunchbox. I lost it in an accident recently, and here it's being auctioned off. It's precious t' me, and I need your help t' get it back."

Bent ignored him as he was going through the paper avidly. "Jeez...Was Hitler really a lesbian?"

"What about my lunchbox? You gotta tell me where t' find it."

Bent broke off reading and studied him in confusion. "What lunchbox?"

"The one in your paper. It's mine, and I need your help t' find it again."

Bent examined the picture for some time. "Well, gee, I'm sorry to hear about your loss, but journalistic ethics forbid me from revealing confidential sources."

"*What* confidential sources? It's in the paper!"

"Huh? So it is." Bent ignored him and went back to working his way down the column. "Isn't that something?"

"So what's the big secret, anyway? You got this from a press release. Surely you can let me see it."

Bent gave him a disgusted look. "And how are we supposed to get exclusive scoops if everyone goes reading press releases? You think those are for public consumption or something?"

"So how did you learn about Hitler, huh?"

Bent looked up in surprise. "What about Hitler?"

"He's a lesbian?"

"Oh. *That's* in *all* the papers. Don't you read?"

"LORD, SO *MANY* STRAIGHT LINES!"

"Look, can you help me or can't you?"

Bent pondered him for a long moment with a calculating eye. "Sorry. I can't reveal that the auction is being held today at 'Dewey, Cheatham & Howe', right here in this city. Journalistic confidence, you understand." He dropped the paper and began doodling casually on an index card as he spoke. "And of course I couldn't tell you 'Dewey, Cheatham & Howe' is the most exclusive private auction firm whose clientele would go righteously ape-shit if mere commoners turned up there. Nor could I reveal that you'd never get past the front door if you aren't on their invite list."

"But what about my lunchbox? It's precious t' me!"

"That's the tragic thing about all this. Can you *imagine* the sensational headlines if a big outfit like 'Dewey, Cheatham & Howe' was caught fencing stolen property?" He finished his doodling, an address, dropped on the paper and folded it again.

"Stolen property?"

"It sure looks that way, doesn't it? Shocking!"

"Scandalous, huh?" Uberbubba said, skeptically.

"Ain't the word for it! Can you *imagine* the spectacle if someone got past their security by going through the service entrance in the alley? If their security guard, Schmidt, was bribed with a twenty dollar bill? If the auction was interrupted right there on the floor by the rightful owner of a stolen item? Good heavens! It'd be the scoop of the year!"

"Big news, huh?"

"A Pulitzer for damn-sure!"

Uberbubba eyed him suspiciously. "Yeah, I guess it would be."

"It's a shame about your lunchbox," Bent mused as he handed the paper back with the index card folded in it. "I'm sure Olsen here knows what I'm talking about. Don't you, Jimmy?"

Olsen was a skinny Goblin, little more than a gangly kid, with a huge box camera draped around his neck. "I sure do, boss!" he said with a shit-eatin' grin.

§

## "Door Number Three..."

"That's the place." Olsen pointed at the imposing facade of a large building just down the street.

"This better work," Uberbubba said, sullenly. "I had t' max out my Visa card t' get this-here twenty."

"Hey, it's only money. Speaking of which, being a news journalist is thirsty work..."

"I bought you three Icy-Colas already. You can do without for a few minutes."

"Cheapskate!"

Their destination *was* imposing: a solid monument of marble with Roman columns across the front, and a discreet bronze plaque by the entrance which read:

### Dewey, Cheatham & Howe
#### Auctioneers By Invitation Only

"Some fancy digs, huh?"

"I don't much like their look." Elvin nodded toward two security guards on either side of the main entrance. They were identically dressed in charcoal grey suits, narrow ties, polished black shoes and wrap-around sunglasses, and wore discreet earphones with wires vanishing down into their collars. Their heads turned as one to follow them on down the sidewalk.

"Creepy barstids," Uberbubba said.

"Yeah." Olsen seemed nervous. "They come out'a nowhere, too. You do somethin' and they'll be standing right behind you."

They moseyed on down to the end of the block, and tried to act casual as they sized up the entrance to the alley. Olsen looked all around to see if anyone was watching. "Can't be too careful," he mumbled. He gestured furtively, and they crowded into the entryway in a rush, pushing and cursing and knocking over a trash can with a loud clatter.

"Brilliant, people!" Olsen swore when he caught up with them. "It's a wonder you don't have the entire city down on us!"

"They couldn't all fit in here, could they?" Dotty asked.

"*That'd* be a story! Come on, let's move."

112

The alley was dark and narrow, cluttered with odd trash and the occasional passed-out wine-o. About half way down, they came to a solid steel security door set at street level. A sign on the door said, BEWARE OF DOG.

"Oh, really?" Uberbubba griped. "That old gag?"

"What is black and brown and looks good on a Redneck Elf?" Elvin asked, rhetorically.

"Dobermans!" they chorussed.

"Love you too. So how do we break in without settin' off any alarms?"

"With your head bash it in perhaps you can?"

"Nah, that would make too much noise."

"YOU COULD JUST TRY KNOCKING."

"Maybe you could climb in the window?" Dotty suggested.

"Yeah! Good idea...except...there's no windows."

"You might try that crowbar laying conveniently nearby." Stapledon pointed to a crowbar laying conveniently nearby.

"Hmph! Ain't that convenient!" Uberbubba retrieved the crowbar and wedged it into the door frame as best he could, then grabbed the knob to steady himself...

...the door opened; the crowbar slipped and landed on his foot. "OW! Dammit, it's unlocked!"

"Brilliant he is," Yokel said, sarcastically.

"HE'S A NATURAL."

"A natural what?"

"INDEED."

The inside was gloomy, dusty, and dark as a tomb. In fact it was a tomb: there were several sarcophagus, some ancient Egyptian grave goods and some creepy-looking tombstones among the antique furniture and assorted oddments. "You see anyone?" Uberbubba whispered as he scanned the gloom.

"Well, I see you."

"Elvin I see too."

"BUT YOU CAN"T SEE ME, WHICH IS REASSURING."

"Stapledon? Where are you?"

"Right here beside you."

"Oh..."

"*Don't* start that again, people!"

They moved out, clinging to each other nervously as they crept along, watching in all directions for any sign of danger. There was a fluttering sound, and a bat flew low overhead. "This place'd make a great haunted house," Elvin muttered as a figure wrapped head to toe in bandages went shuffling past.

"Or a set for a cheesy-ass B movie," Uberbubba replied. The whole place was festooned with cobwebs and drop cloths, and the air was close and dank. There were faint strains of sinister music playing somewhere in the background.

"Frightened you are?" Yokel asked.

"Naw, not really. This place is kind'a cool...WHOA!" He rounded a corner and all but ran into another grey-suited security guard. "...Now *that's* scary!"

The guard looked him up and down, and clearly wasn't impressed. "The great Uberbubba himself," he said, chillingly. "We meet at last."

"And you are?"

"Schmidt. Agent Schmidt."

"THEY ALL LOOK ALIKE TO ME."

They did: this Agent Schmidt was a carbon copy of the two out front. "It seems you've been leading *two* lives," he said, ominously. "One life as a drunken wastrel in the Bayou, and the other as the supposed savior of the Elves. Neither of these lives has a future. You've been living in a dream world if you think you'll ever be a hero and get the girl."

"Hey, it's not my fault I got a problem that way."

Schmidt raised a skeptical eyebrow. "You could take a blue pill for that."

"Yeah, except those ones I got from Mexico didn't work."

Agent Schmidt shrugged. "Tell me, mister Uberbubba, what purpose brings you here?"

"*Mister* Uberbubba? Oh, you mean me? Um...what makes you think I have a purpose?"

"You must have a purpose, for we all know without purpose life has no meaning."

"Never been t' the Bayou, have you?" Elvin said.

114

"Um...well...I'm lookin' fer the owner of this-here twenty dollar bill." Uberbubba held it just out of reach. "I'm sure he's in here somewhere."

Schmidt focussed on the twenty. "I'm going to help you, mister Uberbubba, whether you want me to or not." He snatched the twenty and walked off, disappearing into the stacks of auction items.

"They are *so* damned predictable," Olsen grunted. "It's like they were programmed or something."

"He's a real Knowitall Buttinski, ain't he?" Elvin said.

Uberbubba agreed with *that*. "Glad t' be rid of *him*. He gives me th' creeps."

"*You* should talk." Olsen pointed to some lights in the gloom ahead. "There's the way to the auction floor. I'm gonna get set up. When your lunchbox comes up, you make your move."

They headed for the light while Olsen steered off to the left and vanished into the shadows. The light came from a door leading into a short hallway, which emptied in turn into the lobby. They stopped right at the end.

"Hokey-dokey." Uberbubba peeked cautiously around the corner. The lobby was crowded with distinguished-looking people being escorted in by hordes of uniformed ushers. There was no way in hell they could get to the auction room without being spotted. "The entrance is right there. Everyone act natural."

They gathered what little self-possession they could and broke from cover, trying to look natural as they sauntered toward the main entrance while feeling about as obvious as a buffalo stampede. They made it past the palm trees...along the windows...past the decorative guide ropes...and reached the entrance where the guests were flowing past. For once their lowly status worked to their advantage: the rich and powerful deemed them unworthy of notice, so they were able to blend into the traffic flow while their betters studiously ignored them.

It almost worked. They reached the door to the auction room before they were confronted by the concierge, a large Troll in a cutaway waistcoat and striped trousers, who looked them over with obvious distaste. "And *where* do you think *you're* going?"

There comes a time in every person's life when they face the ultimate challenge, and must either rise to the occasion or fall in disgrace. Mercifully, one of Uberbubba's chief skills was B-S-ing his way out of trouble, and disgrace was an old friend; he rose to the challenge without a quiver. "I'm here fer the auction," he breezed. "I always wanted one of them Howdy Doody lunchboxes, and I intend t' get this one."

"Do you now? I'll have you know this is a *private* auction reserved for the *wealthiest* and most *distinguished* patrons!"

"It damn-well *better* be! I don't go throwing oil millions around in any ol' thrift store!"

"Is that so?" The concierge stuck his hand out. "May I see your invitation, please?"

"Invitation? Oh...um...silly me." He made a show of checking his pockets and going through his waistband. "I must have left it in my other suit."

"You have another suit?" Dotty wondered.

"And you *certainly* cannot come in here dressed like *that!*"

"This *is* Casual Wednesday, ain't it?" Their assortment of dirty white pants suit, bib coveralls, tatty hooker outfit and a layer of green mold couldn't help but stand out from the crowd.

"Casual Wednesday was *yesterday,*" the concierge sniffed.

"Um...well, you know how it is: I get so busy with all them big multi-national deals, I just plum forget the time."

The concierge studied him suspiciously. "You aren't a Redneck Elf, are you?"

"Ah...um...well...now you mention it, I'm..."

"Ambassador from Boo-la Boo-la this is," Yokel said. "Dressed in native garb he is. Respect their ways you should."

The concierge studied Uberbubba skeptically. "*This* is the Ambassador from Boo-La Boo-la?"

"And never so insulted in his life he is! A diplomatic incident you would create? Think you an embargo to start? Think you to cause a nation-wide shortage of loofahs?"

"*What* loofahs?" the concierge protested. "We have standards here! My duty is to keep the riff-raff out, so I need to know if he's a Redneck Elf."

"Well, really, I'm...OW!"

Elvin kicked Uberbubba's shin to shut him up. "He's upset that you'd say such a thing! Can't you hear his pain? It's a mortal insult! Wars have started for less!"

The concierge turned pale. "*Wars?*"

"Your statement is a flagrant violation of the Civil Rights Act," Stapledon commented. "Your accusations denigrate this individual, imposing a sense of shame and self-loathing..."

"*What* self-loathing? Just because I'm a...*OW!*"

"Now you've done it! These negative stereotypes have retarded his emotional growth, which manifests itself as pain spasms in his shins. This could easily turn into an epic class-action lawsuit..."

"Whatever!" The concierge threw up his hands in despair and walked away.

"Saved your sorry ass again have we," Yokel lectured Uberbubba once he was gone. "Enough bad habits already I have."

"BUT THIS ISN'T NEARLY AS MUCH FUN AS SOME OF THEM."

"Yeah, you owe us *all* for this one," Elvin kvetched.

"Oh, look. The auction's started." Dotty pointed down the aisle to the podium. Uberbubba's lunchbox was on the stand, and the bidding was hot and heavy.

"My precious lunchbox!"

"Yeah, well it's now or never," Elvin said.

"Damn straight!" Uberbubba charged down the aisle, determined to put a stop this travesty before the end of the page. He was almost to the podium when Olsen popped up from the side and fired his flash, blinding him...

The hammer descended. "SOLD for three million dollars!"

...Uberbubba ground to a halt right before the podium, and watched in numb dismay as his precious Howdy Doody lunchbox was packed in a well-padded container and whisked away in an armored car. All the while his mind reeled with the tragic thought that his prized childhood possession was gone forever. *Three million dollars!* He never *imagined* that mangy old piece of tin was worth so much. With that kind of loot he could have bought the hugest, fanciest, most luxurious triple-wide motor home *ever!*

"M-my lunchbox," he whimpered as the crowd disbursed. "My precious...gone..."

"Man, you in heartbreak hotel, ain'tja?" Elvin bellyached. "What a friggin' waste."

"All for nothing this farce was."

"WELL, WE HAD A FEW LAUGHS ANYWAY."

"Yeah, an' that concierge feller is cute," Dotty gushed.

Olsen came by just then, and gave Uberbubba a disgusted glare. "Pal, you're as useless as teats on a boar hog. I'm all lined up for the scoop of the century, and you had to freeze!"

"Sorry. Your flash blinded me."

"Oh, yeah. Blame the media!" He flipped Uberbubba off and headed up the aisle grumbling, "Another damn Pulitzer blown to hell."

§

## "The Answer Is..."

They wound up back on the street in front of the auction house. Uberbubba sulked while the others stood around watching the scenery or gossiping among themselves. He was thoroughly fed up by then after being dragged away from his life in the Bayou, put through hell, his Visa maxed out, and his precious Howdy Doody lunchbox gone forever. "It sucks bein' a Messiah," he sighed.

Dotty noticed him at last. "Sorry about your lunchbox," she offered. "It was all old and rusty anyway."

"And worth three million bucks! I could'a bought the whole damned Bayou fer that much."

"Um...why do that?"

"What now will you do?" Yokel asked.

"I dunno. Go home, I guess."

"WHAT ABOUT THE HIGH ELVES? YOU STILL HAVE TO REUNITE THE KINDRED, YOU KNOW."

"Don't be cruel," Elvin complained.

"Damned if I care," Uberbubba grumbled. "I don' know why I should bother." He sulked for a bit, then, "But I'm still stuck with this damned Prophecy, ain't I? I gotta dump it if I'm ever t' get Jimminy Cracker t' quit mooching my White Lightning. Only I'll be switched if I know what t' do next."

"This whole quest was a fool's errand right from the start," Stapledon commented. "The prospect of a Redneck Elf saddled with the Prophecy he was never intended or equipped to bear violates every principle of Karma, the Cosmic Yin And Yang, and the whole idea of Divine Intervention..."

"Whatever!" Elvin and Dotty chanted.

"No...wait..." Uberbubba finally had a clue. "You're the guy what has all the answers. You tell me: how do I reunite the kindred?"

"So you finally see why I was stuck in this mess." Stapledon preened himself in his moment of glory. "To answer your question, you can't. The High Elves are too alienated from the social matrix to be mainstreamed, and the Low Elves are too mired in stupidity and their insular ways to ever change. And then there's the Redneck Elves...well, enough said there. I hate to be the one bearing bad news, but your whole quest was for nothing."

"Great!" Uberbubba shouted. "Now we can forget this stupid save-the-Elves bullshit, and get on back home!"

"Disappointed I am," Yokel sighed.

"BUT NOT SURPRISED."

§

### "Get The *Fuck* Out-a Dodge"

They wound up on the Yellow Line bus headed back to the Greyhound station. Uberbubba was in a funk, wondering what he could do now that his quest had failed. "I'm screwed!" he wailed. "I'll never be free of this damned Prophecy."

"Blame not yourself," Yokel offered. "Upon a Redneck Elf the Prophecy was never intended to be. Destined to fail you were."

"IT'S ALL PART OF A PREDICTABLE PATTERN."

"Yeah, don't go writin' a sad song over it," Elvin said as he tried a few chords on his electric guitar.

"Indeed," Stapledon commented. "Your prospects are fatally impeded by your socio-economic background and limited education, which preclude any hope you might have of ever..."

"Whatever!" Uberbubba brooded for some time, going over recent events once again. "Still...I couldn't have done it without you guys t' help."

119

"Since nothing we accomplished not surprising this is."

"WE SURVIVED, SO IT'S NOT LIKE WE ACHIEVED NOTHING."

"Surprising *that* is!"

Uberbubba caught a familiar sight through the smog outside. "There's our stop." Without thinking, he headed for the door while the others, also not thinking clearly, followed him. It was only after they were off the bus and it left that he realized his mistake. "Shit, we're still in the 'hood."

"Got off the bus too soon we did." Yokel was alarmed to find they were at the same stop they started from earlier, deep in High Elf country.

"SPEAKING OF FATALLY IMPEDED, HERE'S PROOF IF YOU NEED ANY."

"This ain't th' Promised Land," Elfin said.

"What d' we *do?*" Dotty whimpered.

Uberbubba looked nervously at the High Elves gathering around them. This wasn't good. "We walk, nice and easy," he muttered. They started casually walking uptown, but their way was blocked by a surly mob of High Elves. "...or perhaps we'll go that way." They changed course, and tried to urgently saunter across the street, but were cut off again by another gathering mob. "...or not. We might try that way instead." They broke into a panic-stricken amble the other way, but were cut off again as the High Elves closed in around them, forcing them back to the wall where the Terrible Twos were sitting.

"You back again, huh...?" the one on the left said.

"...you been tol' you ain't welcome here..." the one on the right added.

"Sorry," Uberbubba said, warily. "Wrong stop. We're just passing through."

"Well you better get a move-on..."

"...'cause we don't like your kind 'round here."

"Um...sure. Anything you say." They aimed nervously up the street toward the distant Greyhound station, and for a moment the crowd drew back to let them pass, but as sure as sunrise, one of Uberbubba's *many* failings was his complete lack of the instinct to shut the *fuck* up and move along. He paused and turned to the twins. "So...did you ever decide which of you is which?"

"What you want t' know that for?" the one on the left growled as his eyes narrowed.

"Yeah. You gettin' some kind-a *deviant* ideas or sumpthin?" the one on the right growled as the tone of the High Elf mob turned ugly.

"Um, hey, I was just asking..."

(both) "And we're just sayin' *No Way*!"

"You have challenged their masculine self-image," Stapledon commented. "They are about to go into a gay panic and do something regrettable which, regardless of the testimony of numerous and very expensive expert witnesses, will not serve as a defense later..."

"What*ever! Jeez!*"

"Did it now you have," Yokel muttered.

"YES, SHIT-FOR-BRAINS STRIKES AGAIN. WHY AM I NOT SURPRISED?"

"We ain't gonna have your kind-a *pre*-version goin' on 'round this 'hood..." the one on the left yelled as the mob closed in on them.

"...you pokin' your noses in where you ain't welcome..." the one on the right added.

"...and we're gonna do sumpthin' about it..." The one on the left clambered down off the wall and grabbed a piece of pipe.

"...we're gonna show you what we think of *your* kind..." The right one joined him, producing a vicious-looking switchblade.

"...you're gonna pay the price..."

"...for earning the wrath of YoMamma!" they finished together.

Dotty seemed to come out of her perpetual haze and looked them over contemptuously. "So, a fine pair of bullies you are!" she hissed. "Love inflicting pain, do you?"

"Crush your fingers!..." they replied with evident relish.

"...rip out your eyeballs!..."

"...tear your skin off!..."

"...tickle you..."

"...then tear your skin off!"

She staggered to the middle of the pack, confronting the Terrible Twos, hands on hips. "You two are really disgusting. Love to pick on helpless weaklings, eh?"

"Helpless..."

"...weak, yeah." They were drooling, more than usual.

"See 'em cringe..."

"...hear 'em beg for mercy..."

"...but no mercy! 'Cause we love it!"

She was undismayed by their ghoulish delight. "And I guess you'll want the weakest and most helpless first, won't you?"

"Weakest..."

"...Yeah." They were slavering in anticipation.

Dotty made a quick backward jab with one foot, her 6 inch spiked heel catching Bob-Leroy-Billy-Leroy-Bob squarely in his tender parts. He went down with a squeal and curled up in a ball, clutching himself.

"Someone even weaker than us, I'd think."

"...uh, YEAH!" Their eyes focused on Bob-Leroy-Billy-Leroy-Bob with obscene glee. "Let's start with him!"

The High Elf mob descended on Bob-Leroy-Billy-Leroy-Bob with a bloodthirsty roar and carried him bodily up the tenement steps, forgetting their intended victims in their excitement.

"But guys!" Bob-Leroy-Billy-Leroy-Bob gasped. "I'm yo brother! What'll YoMomma say when she finds out?"

"She don't gotta find out nothing..."

"...and you won't be telling her, snitch!"

They vanished through the doorway, and a horrible shriek came floating out a moment later, followed by the renewed blood-roar of the mob.

"Come on! We're out'a here!" Dotty grabbed UberBubba and Elvin, who were headed toward the door after the mob.

"Leave here we must before wise up they do."

"FORGET THEM. TIME TO DUMP THE BAGGAGE AND BOOGIE."

"NO! You can't leave my little Tote!" Dotty reversed course abruptly and grabbed her travel bag.

"NOT THAT! THOSE TWO MORONS!"

"You can't ask me to give up my little Tote," she blubbered. "That's inhuman!"

"WHATEVER. WE NEED TO HUSTLE."

Yokel, Stapledon and Dotty set off up the street, with Tote squeaking "Yip! Yip! Yip!" along behind. "It's all right, little Tote," Dotty simpered. "We won't let those *nasty* people get you." Uberbubba and Elvin, realizing they were being left behind, hurried to catch up, pursued by more hideous screams and the roar of the mob behind them.

§

**"The Parting Of The Fellowship"**

Somehow they made it back to the Greyhound station without getting lost more than once or twice in ten blocks, and went to ground behind the vending machines. "I think we lost them," Uberbubba said at last as they watched the columns of black smoke and the news helicopters hovering in the distance.

"Through no fault of ours are we saved." Yokel was following the live coverage on the station TV monitor. "Search for us they still do. The wit they lack to seek us here."

"THANK HEAVEN FOR INBREEDING."

"Gee, that looks ugly." Uberbubba watched the coverage in dismay. Several blocks of the Big City were burning, and National Guard troops were moving in amid clouds of riot gas. "Hey, ain't that th' Greyhound station?" A swift pan shot from a passing helicopter showed his Little Red Wagon parked in the front lot.

"Yeah," Dotty said. "We're on TV. Ain't that something?"

"Cool!" Uberbubba scuttled out into the parking lot and began waving and jumping up and down. "Heyyy everyone on the Bayou! It's meeeee! Uberbubba! Here I am in the Biiiigggg Ciiityyyy!"

"He'll show them where we are," Elvin grumbled.

"Which will be catastrophic," Stapledon commented. "Right now the Terrible Twos are on a rampage searching every hiding spot and bolt hole for blocks in all directions. The High Elves are in a full-blown gay panic, in fact, and sociologists are already warning the government that the rioting could spread..."

"Whatever," they chorused.

They watched in silence as riot police and National Guards tangled with the rioters. A fire truck raced past on the street outside as Uberbubba went on capering and waving excitedly.

"They find us, it won't be pretty." Elfin settled on one of the hard plastic waiting room seats and strummed a few riffs on his electric guitar. "That's a tough audience."

"Stop him before they see us someone should," Yokel said at last.

"WHY? IT'S SOCIAL DARWINISM AT WORK."

The helicopter faltered and turned back. The TV monitor flashed a brief image of Uberbubba capering and waving excitedly, then they cut to a commercial.

"Didja see me?" he asked when he came back in. His face was flushed and he was giggling in excitement. "I was on TV!"

"Your performance Oscar-worthy was," Yokel said.

"HE'LL MAKE THE COVER OF NATIONAL GEOGRAPHIC FOR SURE."

The Station keeper came over just then, backed up by two husky baggage handlers. "Hey, you birds headed somewhere, or do I call the vagrant squad?"

"Um...we're headed for the Bayou," Uberbubba said. "When's the next Greyhound due?"

"Same time they're always due: somewhere between Oh-God-Hundred and T'hell-and-gone. Unless they're late. The ticket booth's right over there." He gave them a contemptuous look and went on his way.

Uberbubba turned to the others, who were studiously ignoring him. "I guess I'm gonna pick up the fare again, huh?" They hemmed and hawed, studied the ground, perused the magazine rack, and too-obviously avoided his gaze. At last he sighed. "Well, we'll stick together anyway..."

"Not me," Elvin kvetched. "I seen enough of the Bayou. I'm gonna get me a steady gig in Lost Vegas."

"And I'll go with you, my big hunk o' love," Dotty simpered. Elvin blanched at that. "You think I want to go back to Kansas?" she complained. "There's nothing there but cows and sheep..."

"Sheep?" Uberbubba's ears perked up.

124

"...a-and it's all in black and white anyway, real grainy. That's no place for a promising young girl."

"On what you are promising that depends."

"I WON'T TOUCH *THAT* ONE."

"I'm all shook up," Elvin sighed as he looked her over morbidly. "At least I won't be goin' back to the Bayou." He hefted his red-sequined guitar and headed down the street. Dotty tottered after him with Tote squeaking, "Yip! Yip! Yip!" as they faded into the distance.

"Well, we'll stick together anyway," Uberbubba said to the others as they passed over the horizon. "We'll make a triumphant entrance..."

"Think you so stupid I am?" Yokel said, severely. "Escape my dismal fate I have. My scholarship I will take. To Harvard Law I will go. In hell your stinking Bayou can rot."

"AND I'M GOING BACK TO CENTRAL CASTING. MAYBE I CAN STILL SALVAGE MY CAREER."

Uberbubba watched impassively as Yokel The Wise Hermit (no comma) hobbled down the crumbling sidewalk and out of the story. Then he turned to Stapledon, the only one left of their Fellowship. "Well, we'll stick together anyway..."

"Like hell," Stapledon commented as he faded into the wallpaper. "I hear there's another Star Trek movie in the works. They'll need me to provide info-dumps for background and technical stuff, off-site plot developments, history, and a lot of other things you would never know otherwise..."

"Whatever."

And so it came to pass that the Fellowship were sundered as they bailed out, boogied, took a powder, rode out on Shank's Mares, or just discretely faded into the background. At last Uberbubba was alone, killing time munching candy bars from the vending machines as he watched the riot on the station TV monitors until night settled.

It was early in the morning when the Station Keeper shook him awake. "Hey buddy, your Greyhound's here."

"Huh? Wha' time-zit?"

"Two in the AM, of course. You want this Greyhound or not?"

125

"Yeah, yeah, okay. I'm up." Uberbubba crawled out of the hard plastic chair he was sleeping in, stretched to get the kinks out of his back, and limped out to the parking lot where his Little Red Wagon was being hitched to a Greyhound.

"Some night, huh?" the yard attendant said as he finished the last connections. He gestured to the nighttime sky to their north, which glowed bright smoky orange.

"Shit, they're still at it, ain't they?"

"Yeah. There was some guy on TV a while ago saying how the High Elves are in an all-out gay panic..."

"Whatever." Uberbubba plopped wearily in his Little Red Wagon. "I'm out-a here and back to the Bayou."

The Greyhound considered him morbidly, and whined.

No sooner did he pull out of the lot than he was cut off by flashing lights as a police cruiser pulled up next to him. The Greyhound panicked and bolted, dragging him on a wild chase down the street. He clung desperately to the wagon rim while police sirens howled after him as they cut through parking lots and up on the crumbling sidewalk. The chase was quickly joined by several more units and a helicopter as he bounced over railroad tracks and squealed around corners to the sound of his tires shredding.

"Whoa, dammit!" he shrieked at the terrified Greyhound, but it only ran faster, dodging a parked car by jumping the curb, almost sending him flying as the police cars howled in hot pursuit.

Several blocks later, a County Ranger vehicle 'Pit'-maneuvered his rear bumper, his Little Red Wagon spun out and crashed into a telephone pole, caving in its right side and leaving him stunned. The Greyhound broke free and took off howling in terror.

"You in a heap o' trouble, boy." The Ranger propped a boot on the wagon's buckled fender and hauled out his ticket book. "You got no tags on this vehicle."

"Tags?" Uberbubba was struck with a sudden premonition his troubles in the Big City were only beginning.

"That's right. You got no lights either. And let's see your license, registration, and insurance while you're at it."

§

## "There's No Place Like Home"

Somehow, through more blind luck and dogged determination than he realized he had, Uberbubba *finally* made it back to the Bayou. His trip to the Big City was an adventure he was determined never to go through again. His Little Red Wagon was confiscated as a road hazard, which didn't matter since it was wrecked anyway. On top of which he had to do five hundred hours of community service to work off the traffic tickets after his Visa card was cancelled, and his precious three million dollar Howdy Doody lunchbox was just a nagging memory. And as if that wasn't bad enough, he'd lost thirty pounds in the process, which would take *weeks* of concerted effort to gain back. And who was the first person he saw when he arrived back at the door to his humble tarpaper shack on wheels? His neighbor, Jimminy Cracker of course, passed-out drunk on his driveway.

"If you don't beat all," he grumbled.

"Wha?" Jimminy stirred, and managed to sit up. "You, eh? Thot you was gone fer keeps."

"I should be so lucky. I been there and back again, just like the Prophecy foretold, and you can keep it."

"Uuurrrrrppppp!" Jimminy greeted that by barfing all over himself.

It was only then Uberbubba noticed his shack was a moldy ruin. The windows were all broken, half the siding was gone, the roof partly collapsed, and there was evidence of an arson fire in the outhouse. "Whahoppin my house?"

"Huh?" Jimminy Cracker stared stupidly at him for a bit. "The river come up again, only you wasn't here t' move it, so it got flooded out."

What little was left was rank and damp and covered with slime and weeds. An alligator hissed at him when he peeked in the kitchen. At least his year's accumulation of trash was gone.

"Why didn't you move it for me?" he demanded. Jimminy Cracker's place was as good as new; shabby and run down and piled about with trash as always.

"Ain't my problem, boy. Take care o' yo' own I always say."

"Some good neighbor *you* are!"

Still it could have been worse; at least his quest was done. The Elves were beyond saving, not that he cared anyway. The Great Prophecy he was saddled with at birth had been fulfilled. The Redneck Elfin kindred would quit bugging him, and he could go back to his humble life of fishing for engine blocks on the Brown River. He breathed deeply of the miasmic stench of the swamp, and gazed impassively at the dismal landscape of weeds and tangled undergrowth. His was a lousy, stinking sinkhole of a life in a lousy, stinking sinkhole of a place, but it was all his. He was home.

"Well," Uberbubba The Fisherman said at last with a deep sigh. "I'm back."

"Sheee-it."

\*\*\*\*\*

# "The Nightlife In This Town Sucks"

I felt like hell when I woke up. After a long moment of staring aimlessly at the ceiling, I rolled over and looked at the bedside clock. "Seven?" I groaned. "Admit it, boy, you partied last night." Not wisely but too well, it appeared.

After a bit I clawed my way to my feet and stretched to get the stiffness out of my back. The dim light coming through the mini-blinds caught my attention, so I took a peek to see what the weather was... "OWWW! Dammit!" The sunlight was painfully bright. I retreated in haste and rubbed my eyes, trying to dispel the after-images.

It took me a while to realize the sun was in the west and about ready to set. "Seven in the evening? Great!" I'd slept the entire day away. Thankfully this was Sunday, but I'd have hell getting my sleep cycle straightened out for work tomorrow. It seemed I was doing that whole lost weekend thing.

My next thought was that I was hungry, so I stumbled into the kitchen and checked the fridge. There was the celery I bought yesterday, some bean sprouts, carrots, tofu, a potato, and a half tub of strawberries. None of it appealed to me, even though I was starving. What the heck, I needed to eat. I grabbed a carrot and started in...

...it tasted horrible. I about gagged. "What th' hell?" I muttered after spitting it out. "I gotta be sick or something."

Actually I didn't feel queasy, nor particularly hung over; I just was starving, but the things I usually like nauseated me. Still, I had to eat, so I decided to head down to the market to see about some of those liquid power drinks. Maybe if I could get some carbs on my stomach, I would feel better.

The sun set by time I was cleaned up and headed out. I could have caught the bus, but the fresh air helped my woozy feeling, so I decided to hoof it for what I knew to be a pretty fair walk. Perhaps some exercise was all I needed. I'd gone about six blocks when I was deflected a block over by some roadwork. The last of the twilight was fading, and I felt a lot better. Yeah, some fresh air and exercise, and some carbs, was all I needed.

This wasn't the best neighborhood, and I kept my eyes open cautiously. I was passing through a run down small business district mostly boarded up long ago. As I soldiered on, one lighted storefront caught my eye. It was a nondescript place with the windows painted over so the only light showing was through the transom over the door. There was a sign:

## *Mephisto*

For some reason it seemed familiar, which it shouldn't have, since I'd never been on this street before. From the name, I wondered if maybe it was some kind of counterculture night spot. Normally I wouldn't be caught dead in *some* of those places around town, but with the bender I must have tied on last night, anything was possible. I had an uncomfortable feeling I'd been here before.

The interior was coolly lit, which was easy on the eyes. While the outside looked like an abandoned slum, the inside was tastefully done like an old fashioned saloon, or maybe a club of some sort; hardly headbanger country. There were comfortable chairs, a couple tables, a sofa, a classic jukebox, a magazine rack and some potted fake flowers. Across the back was a classic bar with a genuine brass foot rail. Instead of shelves of bottles, there were several refrigerators. It took me a moment to notice there was no mirror behind the bar. It must have been early; the place was still empty except for a bartender polishing little shot glasses. It was all very ordinary, but it seemed familiar for some reason.

The bartender looked up when I entered. "Can I help you, sir?"

"Um..." Honestly I didn't know what to say, or why I should bother this guy with my problems, but this whole scene was uncanny. "Maybe you can. Was I in here last night?"

He thought on that for a bit. "Dunno. There was a pretty good crowd in here; I likely missed you." He studied me closely. "You okay, pal?"

"I'm not sure. Had a night last night, ya know? Kind'a confused." Then I noticed his incisors were more like fangs. "So what's with the vampire teeth?"

His smile vanished. "That's poor form around here."

"Whatever." I let it drop, but couldn't help sneaking an occasional peek. Weird dude, what with the dental work.

"Come to think of it, you do look familiar." He pondered me for a moment. "You were with Marcella last night, weren't ya?"

"Um...yeah. I think so." I vaguely recalled a chick I picked up somewhere, although I couldn't pick her out of a lineup now.

The barkeep sighed. "That dumb broad is no *end* of trouble." He considered me for a minute, then said, "You gotta understand this is a private club for a, ah, *distinctive* clientele. You shouldn't have been let in. The bouncer must have missed you." He studied me for a bit, then said, "I guess you better see Mister Big."

"So what? I'm in trouble or something?"

The barkeep offered what he must have felt was a reassuring smile. "It's not like you think. It's much worse." He left off his glass polishing and led me down a short corridor to the back room, me wondering all the while if the place was mobbed up or something. There are lots of ways to feel uneasy, and I was feeling all of them.

§

"Hey boss? We got a donor came wandering in off the street. He looks t' be another one of Marcella's pickups. I thought you'd want to see him."

The back office wasn't what I expected. Instead of goons in Italian suits, there was one elderly gentleman, extra large, with a neat grey beard and receding hairline. He was dressed in conservative tweed, and sat in a comfortable recliner when the barkeep knocked on his door.

"Indeed?" Fat Boy seemed surprised, and looked me over curiously. "Well, let us not be found wanting as hosts. Please come in, sir." He gestured me to a second recliner opposite his while the barkeep withdrew. I slid in uneasily and looked around. The place was wood paneled, with an old fashioned roll top office desk in one corner, a bookshelf, a mini refrigerator, some framed paintings, a couple recliners, and some padded chairs around one of those fake electric Franklin stoves. The lighting was subdued, but comfortable. The whole place was comfortable, in fact. Homey.

"Um, what did he mean by 'donor'?"

He waved that away. "Please forgive the rude remark. It's a slang term for...someone who isn't part of our social crowd." He studied me closely. "But then, it seems Frank was in error. Or perhaps you're new? I don't recognize you, and I pride myself on knowing everyone in our little community."

"I...guess I must be new, whatever new is. I've never seen this place before, and I don't know about any community."

"I suspected as much." His ingratiating smile was spoiled by a wicked set of fangs. "You don't know what happened, do you?"

"Um...no...what happened?" As if I wanted to know.

He opened the small refrigerator and produced one of those old-fashioned glass medical transfusion bottles, opened the valve, drew a shot glass full of something bright red, and set it on the coffee table in front of me. "Are you hungry? You want some, don't you?"

I didn't know what to make of this, but I wasn't reassured by his hospitality. That red stuff looked like...the aroma...was wondrous. It called to me, tormenting me. I was ravenous. I picked the glass up and sniffed it hesitantly, then took the tiniest taste. The next thing I knew, I had drained it.

"Such a waste," he muttered, disapprovingly. "It is clear you are no connoisseur, sir."

"What?"

"A fine aperitif is meant to be savored," he scolded me. "One does not 'chug-a-lug' such an offering."

"Sorry. Um, what was that, anyway? Some kind of vegetable cocktail?"

He winced. "Heaven forbid! That, good sir, was blood."

I reacted in horror. "*B-blood!?*"

"Indeed." He sniffed the bottle, then resolutely closed the valve and returned it to the refrigerator. "Type AB-, from an Oriental. It has a fine bouquet with a light, faintly nutty flavor. Very rare."

"H-human blood?"

He nodded. "A select offering."

"H-human blood? Are you some kind'a sicko?"

He frowned at that. "I shall *presume* your comment stems from ignorance. There is more going on here than you realize."

"Um...but...what *is* going on here? Why blood?"

"Not just any blood; Oriental blood."

"Why Oriental blood?"

"It's their diet: low in starch and fats, high in vegetables, very healthful if one can obtain it from a genuine Eastern source...but I do run on. The sin of the connoisseur."

"I don't get it. What does this have to do with me? Why did that...stuff...taste so good?"

Mister Big sighed in turn. "I must apologize for Marcella's behavior last night. It seems she decided to feed on you..."

"*Feed* on me?"

"...yes. She's a vampire, as are we all. Most mortals we feed on suffer no lasting harm, aside from losing some blood. But every once in a while, very rarely, there are those whom the bite of a vampire transforms into a vampire in turn. That appears to be what happened to you."

"A *vampire?* Me? Ridiculous!"

He gestured to a mirror on the far wall. "See for yourself."

I can tell you I was afraid of what I might see in that mirror, but I couldn't help it. "But...there's nothing here. I can't see myself."

"There you have it. Vampires don't show up in mirrors."

I touched my face in disbelief, and felt two sharp points under my upper lip. "Fangs? *I got fangs?*"

"As I said. You are a vampire, thanks to Marcella."

"B-but I'm a vegetarian!"

"Ah! That would explain it."

"What?"

"Marcella's been on a health food kick lately; low cholesterol, you know."

"Low...cholesterol?"

"Fats, lipids, growth hormones; she's really gone overboard into the healthy fare these last few months. She can be quite annoying about it at times."

"Low...cholesterol?"

"We have our health issues just as mortals do." He looked me up and down. "I can see why she chose to feed on you. From your build, I'd say your body fat content is under fifteen percent."

"Ten point nine," I muttered in disbelief.

"Excellent." He nodded approvingly. "You take care of yourself. She must have felt your blood was, shall we say, health food."

I sank back into the recliner, dazed by this wild tale. I was a *vampire?* These things *just* don't happen except in the movies, only I had fangs. *He* had fangs. *Everyone* I'd met here so far had fangs. And from what he'd told me, there was a lot more to this than some creepy old Bela Lugosi flick. This whole scene creeped me out something awful, to say nothing of how he looked me over. "So...what is this place? A bar for vampires?"

He mused on that. "Think of it as more of a restaurant and social center, like one of those trendy sandwich shops. I am pleased to say 'Mephisto' is an old, established firm with an esoteric clientele."

"Esoteric ain't the word for it! You got some kind'a devil worship thing going on here?"

He chuckled. "Oh, hardly. The name's a little play on our reputation among the donors."

"Uh...um..." What does one say at a moment like this? I struggled to grab hold of something I could relate to... "Um...health food? This is...healthy? You...don't..."

"True. I take dreadful care of myself, I'm afraid." He sighed and shrugged his massive shoulders. "It's my own fault, I suppose. I've always had a weakness for junk food." He caught my stunned expression. "Americans have the *worst* diets; far too much salt and starch."

"A-and s-so...you...drink *Oriental*...?"

"You might say I have cultured tastes. Orientals are fine as a light beverage, or for dieting, but an hour later you'll be hungry again." He sighed once more. "I am terrible when it comes to dieting."

As appalling as this was, I couldn't help being intrigued by this bizarre twist. "Um...what other kinds are there? Latinos?"

He winced. "Too spicy for my pallet. All that chili and hot peppers; they give me gas."

"Gas, huh? Well, what about Afros?"

"Well *real* Africans are excellent; light like Orientals, but with more body. Arabs are too, for the most part, with a fresh, fruity bouquet. It comes from their lean and varied diet, all those dates and pomegranates. Afro-*Americans*, on the other hand, are as bad as Anglos. Greasy. Not healthy. Sadly addictive."

"Junk food," I murmured in disbelief.

"I once sampled an Eskimo: surprisingly light in view of their diet of whale blubber."

I twitched all over at that. "This is too much! Am I supposed to go round biting people on the neck?"

"Oh, one still finds a few of the old school around these days, but most of us shop for food just as you do, unless poverty forces one to take desperate measures."

"...I...you...have...what?...food stamps...for that?"

"Regrettably not, but we're a close-knit community. We help each other, so it's not a big issue. Of course, there are a few...the deviant sort...like Marcella, who prefer to hunt their food."

I was speechless. I sat there stunned, staring at him in dismay. The only sound was the ticking of the wall clock and faint music in the background. The jukebox in the front room. A seventies Disco number.

"Is there a cure?" I asked at last.

He snorted contemptuously. "There have always been charlatans who claimed they could 'pray the Fey away', but there is no scientific evidence that vampirism can be cured. Plus, honestly, few if any of us would want to be. We live a fulfilling lifestyle with a close-knit community of interesting friends, what's not to love?" He opened the refrigerator and took out another of those transfusion bottles. "You do look hungry." He poured two shot glasses. "Would you care for some Indian O+?"

That sent a shiver through me. "I won't do it! If I can't be cured, I'll die! I'll kill myself!"

He shook his head and gave me a morose look. "Such drama. Fortunately that can't happen. Vampires are immortal."

"I can't die?"

"Fraid not."

"Not even if I try?"

"Sorry."

"I can't shoot myself?"

"Wouldn't work."

"Not even with silver bullets?"

"That's for werewolves. Fortunately we don't have any of *them* in this area."

"So what if I refuse to...ah...drink?"

"Trust me, my young friend, many newcomers such as yourself have tried. The hunger pangs get to be too much after a while." He shook his head sadly. "It's not a pretty sight. Hunger brings out the animal in anyone, vampire or not. A starving vampire is a...you'll excuse the phrase...a bloody nuisance, so we have resources to help those unfortunates who can't adjust."

"What? You're going to force me to drink blood? You got some kind of thought police thing going?"

"Actually it's more like mutual self-help," he explained, patiently. "There are programs, therapy, counseling, support groups. We have a group which meets here once a week, in fact. If alcoholics can do it, why not us? Trust me: when you get hungry enough, you will welcome their help."

"But...drinking human blood? That's gross!" I tried to come up with some rational answer to this insane situation, with no luck. "Um... What if I just stick to animal blood?"

"One *could*, I suppose," he said, severely. "If one is into *that* sort of thing. But it's not something we talk about in *polite* circles."

"But...but...what about garlic? What about a stake through my heart? There's got to be *something!*"

"You're mixing up your Hollywoodisms. Garlic doesn't kill vampires, it only annoys us...our keen sense of smell, you know. And as for a stake, that only renders us dormant for a time. In any case, as the old saying goes, you can't drive the last stake in yourself."

I felt defeated by then. "So I can't even die?"

136

"Nope. You're fated to live forever in robust health." He lifted his glass in a toast. "My sympathies."

"But...what can I *do?*"

"The only thing you *can* do is accept the truth of your condition. You are a vampire, and you will always be a vampire. Only by acknowledging it can you find peace with yourself."

"So what? I can turn into a bat and fly away?"

"A bat has an eight inch wingspan." He patted his bulging stomach suggestively. "How far do you suppose a three hundred pound bat would get?"

That left me in a funk for a bit before I began to see other problems with this mess. "How am I supposed to explain this to my friends? How am I supposed to go to work? I can't exactly do transfusions in the company cafeteria."

"Well for one thing, you can forget the old nine-to-five. You may have noticed how the sunlight bothers us?"

"Yeah. It hurts."

"Sadly, we don't tan; we burn, very easily. But the good news is we don't get skin cancer."

"So how am I supposed t' make a living?"

"We have our own economics, what you might call an *underground* economy." He chuckled. "You should be able to find employment. What do you do, anyway?"

"Um...I'm a computer programmer..."

"Ah! There you have it. You'd be amazed how many of us work in IT or telemarketing. It seems almost like telecommunications and vampires were made for each other. Work at home, set your own hours, in many ways an ideal lifestyle."

The conversation lapsed at that point, and we both noticed the muted sounds of a crowd in the main room. "My, how the time flies when one is in a spirited discussion. It seems we're open for business." He struggled to his feet and took a cane in hand. "Don't fret over it, my innocent friend. You're an intelligent young man, you should have no trouble adapting to the lifestyle." He paused and listened to the muted crowd noise. "Why not come out and meet the folks?"

§

There was a fair sized crowd when the Big Guy lead me back to the main room. Honestly, I expected them all to be dressed in tuxedos and capes—the whole scene in black and white like some Ed Wood movie—but they seemed ordinary enough, except for all the fangs. He led me through the crowd, greeting folks here and there right up to the bar, and laid his hand on my shoulder in a familiar gesture. "Frank, our guest is hungry. Fix him up with something, will you? On the house tab. And introduce him all round."

"Sure thing, boss." Frank looked at me. "So, what'll you have?"

"But...I'm a vegetarian..."

Frank gave me a sardonic look. "That so? Well, we got some Rhodesian Dark O+ here, not too heavy, kind'a dry."

"Come now, Frank, let's not be chintzy. This is a time to celebrate." A smartly dressed couple came up to the bar. Both of them had fangs. "We noticed you here with Marcella last night," she said to me. "Welcome to our little social circle. Frank, set him up some of the Polynesian B+."

"Make that all around," he added.

"Gotcha." Frank opened one of the refrigerators, took out the familiar old-fashioned transfusion bottle, set three shot glasses in front of me, and poured.

"Thanks," I said to the lady as I watched him. "It looks like I got a lot to learn."

"Not to worry." She gave me a *toothy* smile.

"I guess I'll have to mind my pennies for a while until I can find a new job."

"So what do you do?" he asked.

"Programming."

His eyebrow inched up. "Do you do web sites?"

"Sure. Java, XML, EPS, PHP, scripts, all that."

They both offered toothy smiles. "Well, this *is* fortunate." He pulled a card out of his pocket and handed it over. It was for a web developer outfit. "If you can start tomorrow evening, we have plenty of work for you."

That was *one* load off my mind, at least. "Thanks."

"Here you go." Frank set a shot glass full of bright red liquid on the bar in front of me. I stared at it for a long moment, steeling myself for what I was about to do. This was gross...but I had no choice...I had to eat...

...Then the *smell* reached me. The Big Guy was right: vampires have very sensitive smell, and the oder—the aroma—was hypnotic. All of a sudden I was desperately hungry. I picked the glass up gingerly, pondered it for a bit, then took a careful taste. It was heavenly. I sipped again, and again, and the next thing I knew, the glass was empty. I set it down and stared at it, bemused, then looked up and down the bar.

"What? No peanuts?"

*****

# "The Hideous Ed"

Yet another in the endless succession of rainy spring days in Seattle. His morning started out as always: staring vaguely out over the lake as the traffic crept along, feeling empty and used up, facing another meaningless round on the corporate treadmill. *'Why do I bother?'* he wondered, as always. It's not like he needed the money, as good as it was, and the adventure he started out on those long years ago was now empty routine.

Marketing Director for a product long past world-wide saturation: about as useless as teats on a boar hog. The golden quest begun those many years past had soured. Where once he gloried in the battle to beat out the competition and spread the gospel around the world, now it was an endless struggle against a declining market and product obsolescence. *'I just don't know what else I'd do,'* he decided, as always. The weather was cool and overcast, more threatening rain than delivering this time of year, although there was a lot of fog on the 520 freeway. It matched his mood perfectly.

The company chauffeur dropped him at the Executive Entrance where he was greeted courteously by company security and whisked up the private elevator to his office. His morning latte and sticky bun were waiting, as always, and he munched absently as he followed the stock ticker on the main screen in the outer office. It was the same thing every day, every damned day. He sighed inwardly, wondering, not for the first time, if he should cash out, take his mistress, and buy a Caribbean island somewhere. It's not like there was any reason to stay: there were plenty of up-and-coming gunslingers who wanted his corner office, and even some of his long-time companions of that long-ago day when they filed the IPO wanted to slit his throat. They didn't need him, and he sure as *hell* didn't care about them any more. The stock was up another 3/10: an extra eighty million or so. Maybe.

While he watched, Walters from R & D came drifting by. Like a lot of them, he still manifested the geek image they cherished thirty years ago, although slacks and turtlenecks were a bit ridiculous at this late date. He came mooching up nursing a large cappuccino and offered a familiar nod.   His casual demeanor fooled no one: he was there for a council of war.

"I'm hearing buzz that Connor is up to his games again," he muttered.  "He wants both our hides, you know."

"Quite the Empire Builder, isn't he?  So what is it this time?"

Walters shrugged.   "The same old: stagnant growth, no new venues to exploit, new broom in Marketing, all that."

Yeah, the same old.   Connor was an ambitious bastard who figured he had all the answers.  He beat his poor drum half to death trying to wiggle into his office suite—or Walters'—or both. Walters had as many headaches as he did, since the product's notorious shortcomings defied R & D's determined efforts to clean it up.  That was the problem for both of them: a crappy product in a saturated trade.   His relentless marketing was the only thing protecting both their jobs.  Both of them were the most vulnerable of anyone around here.

"And I'm getting rumbles he may have his sights on the Old Man's spot," Walters said.  "He must have *something* going if he would dare try that."

*That* was a disturbing vibe.  If Connor felt the Big Boss was vulnerable...  "He's got Board members in his pocket maybe?"

Walters scowled.  "Dunno.  All I'm hearing is echos.  Could mean anything, could mean nothing."

"His dick must drag on the ground if he thinks he can go up against the Big Boss."

There was a time, he reflected sadly, when he was all gung-ho for this daily treadmill.  He used to be one of the Young Turks, the bright-eyed, hyper-competitive geeks who built this monument to corporate self-aggrandizement.   But that was a long time ago. Decades.   He wasn't so bright-eyed any more; clear-eyed and calculating made up for it.  The hyper-competitive geek was now a senior executive, cunning and ruthlessness having replaced youthful idealism.  Where did it all go?  The old fire was faded and the old zeal largely spent, leaving him to face his upcoming 60s with vast cynicism and world-weariness.

"We'll find out, I guess," Walters sighed.   "In any case, he's sharpening his knives again.  Just sayin'."

But for all that, he was the Player's Player: limo, executive office, stock options, the Big Boss on his speed dial, the works. He was one of the survivors who clawed his way to the top of the heap, who breathed the rarified air. This wasn't the first time he tangled with the likes of Connor. The thought of it, and the Beast within stirred restlessly.

"Let him have his little schemes. Let him sharpen his knives. I'll eat him alive." Hell of a note when corporate in-fighting was the best he could look forward to.

Walters nodded unhappily and drifted away. He checked the stock ticker one more time, finished his sticky bun, and walked through the door to his office...

§

*...he had a fleeting sensation of falling...of being wreathed in flames...of a vast darkness...*

§

...the next thing he knew, he was standing on a narrow platform, a flattened peak of rough-hewn rock which vanished into stygian depths below. All around him, beyond the chasm, a vast cave rose until its ceiling was lost in the burning gloom above. The ceiling was hung with enormous stalactites which glowed an evil blue, and the air around him danced with blue flames.

Opposite his narrow perch, across a thirty foot chasm, was a shelf cut into solid rock with the entrance to a tunnel behind it. To his horror, two *creatures* stood on that ledge watching him. The larger one must have stood ten feet tall, with bowed legs, an enormous beer gut, arms ending in huge clawed hands dragging on the ground, horns on its forehead, and vast bat wings overall. The other was the same, if a bit shorter. Both had glowing eyes, darting forked tongues, and bright blue flames flickering over and around him.

"Wha? What happened? Where am I?" He cringed as the cavern was lit by a vast fireball which emerged from the chasm and washed around him. *"What is this place?"*

"You are beyond any place of your horrid universe," the larger creature rumbled. "Summoned you have been to answer the Ancient Question."

Then he got over his alarm as reality clicked into place. "Damn," he muttered. "Those R & D bastards really went over the top this time." Osgood: of course it would be Osgood. That guy was the geek's geek, always spouting off about bold new horizons of software systems. Frankly he made a lot of the Old Guard uncomfortable, reminding them of what they were like back then. If *anyone* could come up with something like this, it would be Osgood.

"Look, I don't know what kind of virtual reality system you clowns cooked up, but this is too much. You hear me, Osgood? You just can't go Shanghai a senior VP into your little games like this!"

"We know not what Osgood is," the larger creature said. "You were summoned here for a noble purpose."

"Noble purpose my ass! If you think you can..." He stepped to the edge of the rocky pinnacle. "...OWWWWW!" He stumbled back as a blast of searing heat washed over him. "That hurt!"

"Indeed. The Barrier protects you from our world. Far warmer this is than your horrible, frozen reality. Touch it not again for your own well-being."

He examined his hands in dismay; they were blistered and red. The sleeves of his jacket were charred, and his face stung. He smelled burnt hair. "This has gone too far!" he said, shakily. "You guys did a great job, but we can't market something which hurts the customers. The liability alone..."

"It understands not," the smaller one said.

"Indeed. It is as I feared. Let it gaze upon the Orb of Comprehension, then."

"What? What do you think you're..."

The large creature held something up where he could see it. It seemed like nothing in particular at first, a cloudy blue-white sphere the size of a basket ball; but it mesmerized him, drawing his gaze, then his attention, then his entire awareness as his consciousness sank into it. And as it did, as his frightened resistance faded, he began to see beyond the cavern. A warren of tunnels and crudely carved rooms spread around them for miles in all directions. And there were more of those *creatures*. They were everywhere, packing the tunnels and caverns like sardines. Some shuffled along aimlessly, going nowhere in particular. Others lay on the hard stone floors, but most simply sat. A few talked, a few fiddled with pebbles or crude tools, but most stared at nothing. It reminded him of the pictures of refugees huddling in the London subways during the Blitz.

Then he began noticing details. There was no furniture, no clothes, no objects aside from loose rocks and a few crude tools. More than that, no one was eating, nor was there any food or water. There were few children, and no small children. His awareness reached the ends of the cave system, and he cast outward trying to see what was beyond it. It took some time for him to realize there was nothing beyond these caves: no surface, no outside. Nothing.

"This...is real?"

"Understand you now at last."

"What...where is this? Is this hell? Who are you people?"

"We know not of hell," the smaller one said. "This is our world. We call ourselves the daemons."

You...summoned me t-to a, uh, demonic...plane?"

"You have been summoned to the Sacred Chasm Of The Eternal Fire, the Burning Cavern Of G'raakk. Far from your own reality you are."

"But why? Why did you bring me here?"

"We seek help from the Mysteries Beyond Our World. Grave is our peril, and we hope for aid from the Microsoft."

"The...Microsoft?"

"Indeed." The larger one seemed almost desperate. "Long have we probed the Mysteries Beyond Our World, searching in vain. Do you know of the Microsoft?"

"I...um..." He was utterly flabbergasted by this strange twist. "Um...yes. I work for them. I'm a senior executive..."

"Executive? Of the Microsoft?" The large one was dismayed. "Be you not...it? The Bill?"

"I told you this was madness!" the smaller one cried. "Dispel it before it destroys us in its wrath!"

"What?" He was stunned and confused. "The Bill? You mean Bill Gates?"

*"It knows the Unspeakable Name!"*

The larger daemon grabbed a bulky scroll and unrolled it. "Dispel it I will..."

Not good. As creepy and unnerving as this...wherever...was, this talk of dispelling sounded worse. Survival instinct kicked in. "Hey! No, wait! I'm not Bill Gates!"

The creature hesitated. "You are not? What are you?"

"Um...m-my name is Ed..." He was interrupted by another rolling burst of blue flame. "...does that have to do that all the time?!"

"The Hideous Ed," the smaller one mumbled. "Dark indeed is this hour. Long will this tale be told in the legend halls of the people."

"But you are of the Microsoft?" the larger one demanded.

"Um...yeah..."

They both seemed excited. "You are of the Tech Supports?"

"Tech Support?"

"Verily. Long have we tried to find the answer to The Crash, the Secret Which Only Tech Supports May Tell. Long have we searched for the Tech Supports, in vain. Tell us the answer, Oh Hideous Ed, and we shall reward you!"

By that point, he was completely flummoxed, but he was finally getting a handle on this bizarre situation. "Um...Okay, so...what do you want with me, anyway?"

"The Program has broken down. The Music Of The Spheres is discordant. Without the Celestial Harmony we are doomed."

"Music Of The Spheres? Look...if your music program is on the fritz, you need to take it up with the third party vendor."

"We know not of the third party vendor," the smaller one said. "Always we have relied only upon The Program."

"*Our* program? Hey, if you've applied our software to something it was never intended for, that voids the warranty..." He was interrupted by a massive earthquake which rocked the cave, sending stalactites crashing down as blue flame billowed out of the depths. "...b-b-but maybe we c-can work with you!" He dropped to all fours to ride out the quake, staring around fearfully as the roof of the cave threatened to collapse. The two daemons flattened themselves against the wall and tried to fend off falling rocks until the quake passed.

"See you now our need, Oh Hideous Ed," the larger one said to him at last. "The failing of the Program undermines the Music Of The Spheres, the very fabric of existence. The Infernal Plane is eroding, collapsing into chaos."

"You say *what?*" He was thoroughly shaken by that point as this bizarre situation was compounded by their confusing non sequitur. "I don't get it. What does our software have to do with earthquakes?"

"The Program is the foundation of all that is," the larger one said, solemnly. "It created the Rock, and carved the First Cavern, where you stand now. It blessed us with this world, and we have added to it by tunneling, all in praise of the glorious Microsoft."

"*Wait* till Apple hears *this* one!" he muttered in amazement. "So...the, ah, Program *created* this Universe?"

"Indeed."

"What? A Universe of solid rock? Why don't you dig your way to the surface?"

They looked at each other in confusion. "What is the surface?" the smaller one asked. "The Rock is everything. Long have we tunneled through it to expand our world. How can there be a world without Rock? Could a Universe exist of nothing but empty space?"

"We wander into the metaphysical," the larger one said. "We have urgent matters to attend to. Can you help us, Oh Hideous Ed? Long have we told the legends of the Microsoft; can you aid us with Your mercy?"

"Um...well..." He tried desperately to get a handle on this weird situation and to think like a Tech Rep. "What...exactly are the symptoms? How did this breakdown occur?"

"For many ages have we tunneled through the Rock," the smaller one said, solemnly. "We mined the minerals, the ores, which we smelted to make tools. We built our civilization to great heights, creating scientific wonders, works of art and profound beauty as ever we tunneled outward to make more living space for ourselves."

"Your whole civilization is in these tunnels?"

"It is."

"The...ah...place seems awfully crowded."

"It is. For time untold we tunneled ahead of our growing population. But then the Crash came, and we could tunnel no more. Our numbers continued to swell, yet we could not carve more space. We sought to sacrifice our future by ceasing to breed, but it availed us not. The passage ways collapse, the caverns crumble, the hardest tools shatter and make no impression. Nought could we achieve while still our numbers grew."

"And now the digging we have already done is collapsing," the larger one added. The Music Of The Spheres decays, and with it our Universe crumbles."

This was *too* wild. An entire civilization existing in a hollow in a solid rock Universe? Interstellar exploration with pick and shovel?

"So what happened to your civilization? All I see are bare tunnels. Where'd all that fancy art and culture go?"

"We gave it back to the Rock. We found that if material possessions were sacrificed, reduced to their raw elements and returned to the Rock, then we could expand our tunnels a short way further. Thus is our world as you saw in the Orb Of Comprehension. We extended our realm until The Crash came upon us, but then we were forced to give back all we had wrought to stave off disaster. But now our resources are exhausted, and the Universe crumbles around us."

"Your...uh...Universe was created by our software? How?"

"We comprehend not, for there are mysteries daemons were not meant to know."

"Long did we ponder the origins of our Universe," the smaller one said. "Long did we seek answers in the Mysteries Beyond Our World. Many derided us as seeking false wisdom, yet we persisted for generations. We have yet to grasp the divine purpose of The Program, but at least we achieved Revelation: we learned of The Microsoft."

"Thus we search into the Mysteries Beyond Our World seeking aid," the larger one added. "Thus we found you."

He stared at them in stunned confusion for a long moment while he absorbed that. These two were some kind of priests seeking their Godhead...on the Redmond Campus? This was so out there as to defy belief. By any rational standard, this *had* to be the shaggiest practical joke in all of geekdom, but there was no denying the evidence before his eyes. These people—this world—existed. As off the wall as it was, who could say what might happen if software from his Universe somehow slipped over into another? Even Osgood would be hard put to come up with something *this* wild. Normally he would dismiss something so ridiculous, R & D wasn't his speciality and there was no denying the facts before his eyes. Best go with the flow for the moment.

"So...um...what system do you use? NT? Vista? XP?"

The two daemons exchanged confused looks. "We know nought of these," the smaller one said. "Always we worshipped that which brought us into being, the mysterious MS-DOS."

"MS-DOS?" He looked askance at them. "You're using MS-DOS to maintain your Universe?"

"*So it was in the Opening, so it is across the Run Time, so it shall be unto the Quitting*; so the legends tell us. The MS-DOS reached throughout the Infernal plane, throughout the span of ages, to bring Order from Chaos. But now the Program has failed! Our existence crumbles!"

"The Quitting is upon us!" the larger one cried. "Save us, Oh Hideous Ed!"

They certainly *sounded* sincere, and frankly he was at a loss for any other explanation. "Um...well...it sounds like you overloaded the system. That early software was kind of skittish; push it too hard and it would simply give up."

MS-DOS? Somehow that clunky old operating system passed through into this...dimension? It...mutated...and became the founding force which brought this Universe into being? No wonder their world was so limited! That was a sobering thought: could something similar have created the earthly Universe? Was the Big Bang really an...*upload?*

"It gave up?" the smaller one cried. "The sacred MS-DOS? Is there nothing you can do?"

"There's only so much any system can do, especially if you repurpose it. It looks like overpopulation has done you in."

"We will give you anything you desire if you will save us! Many riches have we found in the tunneling, gold, silver, jewels. Save us, Oh Hideous Ed, and we will worship you!"

"But MS-DOS is way outdated. No one uses it any more. We haven't supported MS-DOS for years."

The larger one grew angry. "If you are not the Bill, and you are not the Tech Supports, and you speak evil of the MS-DOS, what then can you do to help us?" He hefted his scroll again. "Misfortunate this is. I shall dispel it and try again."

"No! Wait..."

§

*...he had a fleeting sensation of falling...of being wreathed in flames...of a vast darkness...*

§

...The next thing he knew, he was standing in the doorway to his office. He staggered in shock, caught himself on the door frame before he fell flat on his face, and looked around wildly at the familiar setting. Everything seemed ordinary enough. The clatter and buzz of the outer office was mixed with the beeping of his desk phone; all reassuringly normal. He caught his reflection in the window: he was a mess, face and hands red and blistered, his suit charred, his hair singed way back. "God...did that really happen?" he muttered in dismay. It must have. There was no other explanation for his current state.

He stood stock still in the doorway gripping the fame with both hands as he went over those incredible events in his mind. He was actually *Summoned to the Infernal Plane!* These things *just* don't happen...but they did, unless he'd gone completely psycho. But then how to explain his burns? His suit? It happened, all right.

As he began to get a handle on his amazement, his Marketing instincts kicked in, and the implications started surfacing. Those...daemons...were desperate. Their whole race was doomed. MS-DOS: who'd have believed it? They overloaded the software, as incredible as it seemed, and it Crashed. They looked to him to provide the fix, and they would pay *handsomely*...

"Hey, Edwards?" It was Walters again. "I wanted to tell you...*what th' hell happened to you?*"

That shook him out of his bemusement and brought him back down to earth. "I...ah...had an idea."

"It must be a sure-fire idea!"

This was no time for geek humor. Right then his thoughts bubbled with feverish visions of a new market covering an entire *Universe*; of gold, silver, jewels, that Orb Of Comprehension—they'd make a *fortune* off the CIA with *that* one—and...worshipers? Heady stuff.

"I want you to dig up the development files on MS-DOS. We need to bring that antique up to modern specs."

Walters considered him doubtfully. "Why? It's the dinosaur of dinosaurs. Nobody uses it any more."

"You'd be surprised. There's more potential there than you can imagine."

"Well, okay. You say so. We could take a look at it, anyway."

"More than a look!" he said, sternly. They needed to jump before those two daemons got lucky with some Open Source creep. "We need a top priority program to deal with those old issues, and we need it now!"

Walters pondered him for a long moment, no doubt wondering if he'd gone off the deep end. "Um...which generation?" he asked at last. "The final one before we went over to OS/2?"

"No, the original version." Walters' eyebrows crept up in surprise. "I've got ideas for a huge potential new market if we can finally solve that old crashing problem."

"*New* market? For MS-DOS?"

"Yep." His old enthusiasm was inching upward as he contemplated the possibilities. *Worshipers...* That'll take a whole lot of 'splaining, later. "Roust Osgood and his trolls out of their hole. Tell him to clean up the glitches and the expandability problems, and tell him anything goes. This could be a world beater, and a must-have at that. We'll show Connor who's the Empire Builder around here!"

\*\*\*\*\*

# "Vote Of Confidence"

None is so rare as a day in June, at least in the British Isles, where they were enjoying a fine rare spring day, indeed. The weather was mild, with a fresh breeze and fluffy white clouds in a blue sky, and the sun shown brightly on the crowded streets of London. It was a day, in fact, such as used to convince the British that God favored them to be His anointed rulers over half the earth.

The British Prime Minister knew nothing of it, since he was at his desk all morning working on the new Amalgamation Plan. He wouldn't have missed the fine day, had he been aware of it, for the document he worked on was his pride and joy. He went over the endless Clauses and Appendices, jotting a note here and correcting a typo there with what could only be thought of as fatherly affection. He sacrificed most of his political capital for it, but the price was well paid, since it would reverse Great Britain's long decline. It couldn't help but erase the mistakes of the past from the dear voters' minds come the next elections, too, which was doubly satisfying. All in all, it was a glorious day, and he absently hummed a bit of *'Rule Britannia'* as he worked. This was the diplomatic coup of the century which would revive not only the Empire, but his political fortunes as well! Needless to say, he felt he had the world on a string that morning.

He paused to collect his thoughts at one point, and realized he was hungry. It must be near lunch time. He glanced at his watch...

"That'll nae tell ye the time, laddie."

He looked up in surprise, and was even more surprised to see a tiny man sitting on the edge of his pen set. He was a short, chubby figure (relatively speaking) dressed in a green waistcoat and breeches, with a broad brimmed hat and shoes with curled tips. The Prime Minister's first reaction was disbelief; his second was to hit the button on his intercom...

"And ye dinna need yer blooody great sassanach, not that they can hear ye anyway."

He gradually realized the intercom was useless, so he tried the phone. Nothing. He looked around the room frantically, and noticed his desk clock had stopped. So had his watch, and the clock on the wall. This was alarming; he turned to the tiny figure with growing apprehension.

"Who are you? What are you?"

The little man sighed. "Wha d'ye think I am? I'm a Leprechaun, ye barmy fool!"

The Prime Minister was dumfounded. "A Leprechaun? You don't expect me to believe that!"

"Believe or not as you choose, and be damned!"

The Prime Minister studied the little man in disbelief for a bit, but couldn't come up with any other explanation. "What...did you do? Why don't the clocks work?"

"I froze time for a wee bit so we can have our little chat wi'out bein' disturbed." Said Leprechaun idled over to the document on the Prime Minister's desk and stood reading it for a moment. "So that's it, eh? The treaty that'll take Ireland's freedom away."

"It's for a good purpose," the Prime Minister protested.

"Is it, now?" The Leprechaun gave him a hostile look.

"And it was decided in a fair election. The Irish public agreed these islands need to reunite to form a stronger trading block."

"Aye, and a grand affair it was, argued up and down the land. There was some as agreed, and some as disagreed..."

"And the majority agreed. Narrowly, true, but the resolution passed."

"Aye, among the big folk it did at that. But ye didn't think to ask the wee folk, an' I'm here t' tell ye the answer's no."

"No?"

"We dinna wan' t' see Ireland reclaimed by the Crown, an' we intend t' do somethin' about it."

The Prime Minister leaned back in his chair, crossed his arms, and studied the wee figure skeptically. "Do you, now? And seeing that you 'wee folk' aren't registered voters, what can you do?"

The Leprechaun eyed him levelly for a moment (as levelly as their disparity in sizes allowed, anyway), then said, "Ye've heard of Leprechaun's gold, I take it?"

"Aye...um, yes." He thought about that for a bit. "So, you plan to buy Ireland, then?"

The Leprechaun sighed impatiently. "It's not yours t' sell."

He had a point there. "Not that it matters! If you think we shall relinquish the treaty on your say-so, you are sadly mistaken. Great Britain has far too much stake in this..."

"As do ye, laddie!" The Prime Minister halted in confusion. "Oh, we know all about your political troubles, and they matter not a whit t' us. Ye'll be givin' up the Old Sod, and ye'll take your lumps as is only proper!"

"Will I, now?"

"Aye! And if ye don't, we'll be lookin' t' solve the English problem on our own terms once an' for all."

That got the Prime Minister's *'British'* up. "Great Britain may not be the power it once was, but I can *assure* you we are *more* than capable of dealing with any threat you...*wee folk* care to offer!"

The Leprechaun leaned against his desk lamp, crossed his arms in turn, and eyed him mockingly. "D'ye know where Leprechaun's gold comes from?"

For the life of him, the Prime Minister hadn't the foggiest, not that he'd ever thought about it. "I'm afraid not."

"We make it."

"*Make* it?"

"Aye. The most common spell used by the wee folk is one t' transmute any one substance into any other."

The Prime Minister sat up in surprise. "Is that a fact? And you use this...spell...to create gold?"

"No, laddie. We use it t' create fine whisky, an' ye'll never taste the like, I guarantee it! The gold is a byproduct."

"A...byproduct?" The Prime Minister was confused no end. "A byproduct of brewing? Well, I'll be damned."

"Likely." The Leprechaun glowered at him. "We can create anythin' we want, in any amount we need. So that's why ye'll not be reclaiming the Old Sod for your blooody Empire."

The Prime Minister chuckled. "Or what? You will flood the world market with gold? Or with whiskey?"

The Leprechaun eyed him in disgust. "Ye'r whole race are as dumb as tree stumps!" There was an awkward moment, then, "Think it through, man. We can transmute anything to anything, in

153

any amount we desire, but the process tends t' favor the heavier elements; tis the nature o' the beast. We ha' so much gold that it's a plague upon us. It's making the lighter elements that's the problem."

The Prime Minister was bemused by the notion. "Tends to climb the periodic table? I suppose it would...binding forces...yes, it would have to, otherwise you would get a runaway reaction."

"Thankfully not, seein' how much whisky we make."

"So, then, what will you do with all this gold that's a plague upon you if you don't intend to use it against us?"

"Ye great English lummox! Gold is nae the heaviest element on the periodic table!"

"Oh?" The Prime Minister didn't like the sound of that. "What, then?"

The Leprechaun looked him square in the eye. "Plutonium!"

*****

# "They Ate Hollywood!"

"Aw, for Christ's sake, George! Not *another* zombie flick!" Morty dropped the spiral-bound wad of paper, leaned back in his tattered old office chair, and eyed it with a look like a diseased yak just dropped its load on his desk. "*When* are you going to learn that people *hate* zombie flicks? Hate 'em, George. D'you read me?"

George fancied himself another Otto Preminger, even to the jodhpurs and riding crop, which were sadly out of synch with his thinning hair and wiry, twitchy build. He gave Marty his Stern Director Look. "Hey, my movies are profitable, so what'ja bitchin' about?"

Marty was unimpressed. "That's only because you make them so damned cheap." He shoved the offending script back with one pudgy finger. "That's the only reason you survive on the market share dregs you bring in."

"*And* I have name recognition. People know my stuff."

Marty sighed and wiped his face with a paper towel. Los Angeles in the summer was no joy, and his old window air conditioner was on its last gasp. "I got news, bubbie: Stephen Spielburg you ain't. Maybe that crap sold once, but that went out with tail fins and buzz cuts. Hell, man, your stuff goes straight to DVD these days."

"Which cuts overhead even further! Who needs wide screen and surround sound when they can pop one in the player any old time? T' hell with your ten dollar popcorn! I'll tell you what's outdated: the whole damned industry, is what!"

"Yeah? Amazon dot com is all that keeps you going, pal! You ain't even got a cult following!"

"*And* my stuff turns a profit every time. So what's the sad song for, huh?"

"Profit? Yeah, a few percent on a few thousand invested. which don't exactly make you bankable."

"That's your problem! You're the Money Man, and money is money. There's lots like you in this town. You don't want my business, I'll take it elsewhere."

That was a hollow threat, and they both knew it. Morty wasn't exactly in the Big Leagues in Hollywood; he couldn't be called a middleweight, either. In fact the only people who *did* call him were the perpetual wannabes, 'Artistic' nobodies, and washed-up has-beens from the gutters of Hollywood and Vine—people like George. George had been his top has-been for years, ever since Ed Wood took a hike after *'Plan Nine From Outer Space'*. That still stung, since Morty clung to every one of his thin stable of losers like a drowning man. He thought about it for a bit, then came down. "Yeah, I suppose you got a point."

George thumped the desk for emphasis. "Damn right I do! So, why don't you jump on your high horse, gallop over to Beverly Hills, and hustle some of your backers?"

"Well, I gotta tell you, Georgie, my backers are sick of the sight of you. Profitable or not, they aren't going to play."

"Philistines."

"Look, why don't you try something else? You must be sick of doing the same thing over and over. Why not try spy thrillers or courtroom dramas? Maybe I can sell a new you."

George shook his head sadly. "Wouldn't work. God knows I've thought about it, but the budgeting won't add up."

"Huh? Why?"

"Labor costs. Zombies aren't in the Equity, so I can get 'em by the dozen for dirt cheap."

Morty blinked in surprise. "Zat so? You mean they're *real* zombies?"

"Uh huh. Plenty cheap, too, if you know where to look."

Morty pondered that in dismay, wondering where he found... What unnatural... Such a unique... If it could promote... Buzz on the net... If maybe... "Hmph! I wondered how you kept your budgets so low."

"Yep. There's no union scale, no costumes, no makeup, and no speaking premiums. The Labor Board ruled long ago that 'grrrrrr' isn't dialogue."

"Um, what about perks?"

"No spas, no limos, no personal assistants, no publicists, no luxury hotels, nada."

Morty eyed him skeptically. "No stuntmen, either, I take it?"

"Nope. And what's more, no one cares if a zombie gets mangled up, so no labor litigation."

"Ain't that something?"

"Yeah. It's not just the talent, but the support staff as well. The Craft Trades don't own them, so they're easy."

"Um...so no union scale?"

"And it's not only pay. There's no trade jurisdictions, no sick time, no time-and-a-half, no life insurance, no pensions—they're already dead, you see."

"Hah! So you got no labor costs at all, huh?"

George turned a bit pale. "All we have to do is feed them."

"The Zombies Who Ate Hollywood." Morty eyed the script laying on his desk and thought about it for a moment. "Why Hollywood? Wouldn't it be better to use Bayonne, New Jersey? No sense in biting the hand that feeds you...so to speak."

George looked askance at him. "Have you *seen* the air fare to New Jersey?"

"God, the things I do for a living," Morty sighed at last. "I've been hearing some rumors lately. Maybe I can scare up some backing for you up in Marin County."

§

To their lasting amazement, Morty's inquiry to Marin County got a nibble. It turned out to be a case of fortunate timing: his contact had just closed out a four billion dollar deal, and was looking for new horizons to conquer. And while Morty didn't exactly have the brightest shine in Hollywood, 'Marin County' didn't exactly hold it against him. Plus the buy-in was cheap. 'Marin County' took a nickel-and-dime flyer.

"I did it, Georgie, boy." Morty waved the thick contract at him. "I got Marin County to let down like Mana from Heaven."

"Damn..." George studied the first page of the document in wide-eyed wonder. "*Seven* figures! Damn, Morty! You came through like a champ!"

"*Plus* he agreed to give your footage full processing through his state-of-the-art facility. So now maybe you'll have a little faith in your old pal, eh?"

"Hell yeah, that's great! I *hate* messing with those damned chemicals." George grabbed his ball point pen and scribbled his name on the last page without bothering to go through the rest of the wad. "I'll be able to use color film, and I'll be able to hire some *real* actors this time!"

"No more of your one-hit wannabes, huh?"

"*Forget* them!" George eyed the contract cover lovingly. "This'll make us both. With this kind of dough I can deliver the real deal. That'll get your backer to come through for even more in the future."

"It should, yeah. Assuming you deliver."

"Not to worry." George finished signing with a flourish, and handed the thick document back. "The script's all done, and we won't need any sets or special effects, so it'll be a snap."

"I hope so." Morty was having second thoughts about this from George's enthusiasm. "This guy is Big Time. He'll expect results."

"Hey, I'm in my element here. Don't sweat it. All I gotta do is get it made."

§

Easier said than done. Nothing remains a secret for long in Hollywood, and almost before the contract could be faxed back north, Lou Ellen Parks, she of the famously irritating Cornpone Molasses accent, was on it like a duck on a june bug. Sharks could be more forbearing:

> *"The biggest scoop to come out of Hollywood in yeahs is the rumored undead epic 'The Zombies Who Ate Hollywood!', which brings veteran art-film maker George together with the resources and creative talent of a certain you-know-who in Marin County for a spectacular creature feature that promises to out-zombie anything we've evah seen befo..."*

And just like that the buzz was all over Hollywood, to their collective shock and amazement. George was making *another* of his endless zombie dreck...with the backing of Marin County!

*Marin County!* People never named names; they mumbled the phrase like a prayer, and they all knew *who* that phrase meant. Jeez, what got into the guy? How much money did he pour into this bomb? No one knew, since 'Marin County' always was secretive, but *everyone* knew he had no great love for Hollywood. That stoked paranoia the length and breadth of Studio City. What was he...? Why would he...? How could he...? No one knew anything, but they all instinctively agreed there *had* to be something *sinister* about it all.

Rumors spread, dollar figures skyrocketed, panic set in. Everyone knew 'Marin County' just closed out a deal for *Four Billion Bucks!* For the first time since the McCarthy Era, Hollywood tasted real fear. *Four Billion Bucks!* If he put in one percent of it...five percent? *Ten* percent? *More?* The great edifice of Hollywood was shaken to its core by this unexpected and catastrophic tidal wave.

Rumors abounded. Zombie scripts piled up in every producers' office. Spielburg wept! Projects were cancelled! Theatrical and studio stocks plummeted! There was talk of canceling the Oscars, of moving into radio, of going back to Vaudeville! No one knew *how* bad it would be, but everyone agreed that *George*, of all people, with *Marin County's money* could be a disaster of cosmic proportions.

> *"Everyone who is anyone in Hollywood wonders who will get the nod for this yeah's biggest blockbuster production, 'The Zombies Who Ate Hollywood!'. Producer/ Director George, that creative genius of the zombie epic, is as tight-lipped as the Sphinx about who he has in mind, but it looks to be anyone's ball game..."*

The reaction of the talent was every bit as incredulous as the studios, with the added alarm over what being tied to such a turkey could do to their careers. Fear stalked the spas and nightclubs as the Great and Near Great ran for cover. No one wanted to even be *mentioned* in the same breath, to say nothing of actually being cast in it.

Lindsey was rumored for the female lead: she promptly checked back into rehab, and stayed there. Sean was fingered for the leading man: he retired to a remote corner of northern Scotland, swearing he'd never appear in public again. Johnny left on a long sea voyage! Justin joined the Marines! Paris entered a convent! Aw-nold moved back to Austria! Soon productions all over Hollywood were grinding to a halt as the talent scuttled for the lifeboats.

> *"The latest rumors about the new epic 'The Zombies Who Ate Hollywood!' has everyone who is anyone tryin' to climb on board the greatest gravy train to hit Tinsel Town since Ben Hur. Producer/Director George, that bold rising star in the cinematic heavens, is talkin' it up with all the names..."*

While the studios panicked and the talent fled, the technical rank and file were salivating at the prospect of a massive zombie flick backed by 'Marin County'. Zombies might be a plague on the market, but visions of makeup, prosthetics, animatronics and CGI by the *carload* had them salivating. Every effects shop and animation lab in California clamored for a piece of what *had* to be the biggest big-budget effects film in years. *Four Billion Bucks!* Even a tiny fraction of that had to be monstrous! They descended on George like locusts.

§

And how did George handle all the hype and hoopla?

"I don't *understand* these people," he complained to Morty. "How did my modest little zombie flick spin so out of control?"

"Well that's a good thing, isn't it?" Morty leaned back in his brand new office chair and luxuriated in the cool draft of his brand new air conditioner. "Your biggest problem has always been getting publicity. Now they're coming out of the woodwork for you. Your project is sure to be a hit."

"If I find the time to get it done! They're like cockroaches. I'm being constantly annoyed by phone calls and Priority Mail proposals and all those people camped on my door."

"Hey, it's free publicity."

"Publicity! That's another thing. I got that harpy Lou Ellen on my case. The woman's a banshee, and she never lets up. She's on my ass night and day."

"Hey, she's singing your praises, so why are you singing the blues, huh?"

"Some help *you* are! What if she finds out about my secret formula for success, *huh?*"

That struck a disturbing chord with Morty, rekindling his unease about this whole thing. "Well, you just got to be sure she never gets on the set, is all."

§

Then it started going to George's head. They *really* felt that way about him? He sure as *hell* wasn't used to being lionized by the industry. The uproar from the technical houses thrilled him, and overrode the echoes of panic from the studios and talent. But while he appreciated their interest, he knew better than to reveal the secret of his success, so he kept his comments to vague generalities (his plans weren't any more concrete than that anyway) and told them everything was proceeding 'in an orderly fashion'.

That simple disclaimer touched off another round of panic, especially when they learned 'Marin County' would be processing the footage. If the hype earlier was bad, *that* tidbit had them foaming at the mouth. Insiders high and low railed haplessly at 'Marin County's state-of-the-art facilities, *Four Billion Dollar* war chest, their endless string of mega-hits, and their long tradition of secrecy, and wondered what sort of *monster* was about to be unleashed upon them.

> *"Interest in the new epic, 'The Zombies Who Ate Hollywood!', widely seen as the anti-establishment metaphor of our times, is reachin' beyond the inner circles and creatin' no end of buzz on the streets of America..."*

The public reaction was incredulous at first, but as soon as they got over their shock, they reacted. For the first time since Elvis Presley appeared on Ed Sullivan, clergymen around the country besieged the FBI with complaints that this was a threat to national security. The PTAs, Scouts, and 4H organizations railed at 'Hollywood decadence'. There were demonstrations and an investigation in Congress, and it quickly became a partisan campaign issue.

Meanwhile, zombies became the latest youth craze. Before long, the act of randomly biting people came to be called 'zombing'. There were zombie gangs, zombie-theme night clubs, zombie boy-bands. Zombie makeup and jewelry were the top trend items. There was even a chain of zombie fast-food joints; they were swamped with customers ordering 'Fast Fried Freddie' and 'Morgue Munchies'. It spun more and more out of control every day, even making the cover of Newsweek.

§

"Now it's become a political issue!" George railed at Morty. "The freakin' NRA wants my heroes to be armed with *American made* firearms, and they've got their Congressmen breathing on me. You should see all the firepower the gunmakers sent!"

"So? It saves on props?" Morty was getting annoyed with how George paced back and forth in front of his brand new desk, raging at all his problems.

"And that ain't all. The Jewish Anti-Defamation League wants me to include some authentic golems, complete with inscriptions in ancient Hebrew on their foreheads!"

"Um... Zombies are kosher? What did you tell them?"

George looked more stressed than usual. "I managed to talk them down to agreeing that some of the zombies would mutter 'grrrrr' with a Jewish accent."

"I really *have* to see this movie," Morty sighed.

§

That wasn't the worst of it, either. Before long George succumbed to all the hype and hoopla and, filled with feverish visions of the Hollywood grandeur of old, was soon revising his script on a scale he never *dreamed* of in the past. He only had a million to play with, but he was a huckster from way back, and soon he was banging on the door of one of the largest studios in Hollywood demanding access to their storied back lot.

That was greeted with outright contempt until he dropped 'Marin County' and a distribution deal on them, and all of a sudden he had *acres* of period sets for his undead cast to rampage through. 'Marin County' was his personal magic carpet, and it took him to heights which turned his head and filled him with feverish visions of the Big Time.

§

"I tell ya, Morty, it's gonna be huge."  George paced feverishly back and forth in Morty's brand new office, seemingly mesmerized by his sudden fame.  "If they really want this thing to go large, then by God I'll go larger!  I'm made, my man!  You'll see."

"Hey, that's great," Morty said, doubtfully.  "But what about your little secret?  Is that bitch Lou Ellen still riding you?"

"The secret is safe, thank you.  We're shooting everything on the backlot, so no one can get a close look.  Anyway, Lou Ellen Parks is a great lady.  She's beating the drum for me big time.  The publicity is dynamite!"

"You say so."  Morty's uncomfortable feeling was back.  "So when do you start shooting?"

"First thing tomorrow morning."

§

*"The latest word from the studio backlot where "The Zombies Who Ate Hollywood!' is under way is that all is not smooth sailin'.  It seems they'a havin' labor problems..."*

It took weeks of heartache and hassle, but despite it all, George pulled it together in his usual ramshackle low-budget fashion, and started shooting.  But hardly had that begun when the Craft Unions were up in arms over his 'non-union' crew.  It wasn't long before Craft Service picket lines were up, and observers noted (from a distance, since the set was air tight) what a *shabby* lot his crew seemed.  They were an odd mixed lot, dressed in any old clothing —observers stressed that fact—like a batch of dirty derelicts off the street.  They had no safety gear, no tool belts, and no headgear to protect them from the fierce Southern California sun.  Nor did they seem to notice.  Their behavior was odd, too: when they weren't doing something, they would simply stand stock still until called upon once more. No lollygagging, no lounging in the shade, no runs to the port-a-potties; they just stood there. All the zombie extras behaved that way too, in fact, although no one realized the significance of it at the time.

At the same time, observers noted the two lead characters seemed far off their feed in front of the camera. They appeared easily distracted, with numerous retakes and missed cues, although movie wonks noted their reaction to the zombie extras were 'remarkably realistic'.

*"...despite all the headwinds thrown his way by a* jealous *Hollywood, George, that Cinematic Master, is poundin' away on his latest mega-blockbuster 'The Zombies Who Ate Hollywood!..."*

Meanwhile, news items started appearing in the back pages about the mysterious disappearance of homeless and street people. Los Angeles went through periodic bouts of that, it seemed, but no one recalled it ever being so widespread. Dozens were missing every morning. Rumors started circulating about body snatchers or farm labor press gangs or gristly tales of medical organ harvesters. No one knew anything. Everyone was worried. The shelters were soon overflowing, and Social Workers described them as looking like panicked refugees...

§

"I got bad news, bubbie," Morty told him when he arrived at his office in response to an urgent phone call. "Your backer up in Marin County changed his mind. He pulled his backing, which leaves you bupkis." He spread his hands in a humiliated gesture. "You'll have to shut down."

"Huh? What happened?"

"Word is he took a look at your first batch of dailies, and shit himself."

"Sanctimonious clod! What the hell does he know?"

"He's pulled in about ten billion in his career thus far..."

"So? That makes him an expert? That makes him a film critic?"

164

"That makes him the Man With The Money, and he walked...hell, he ran. It's over, George."

"Yeah? Well we got a contract!"

"And he's got all the legal firepower in Hollywood. I went through that contact: there's an 'acceptable standard of production' clause, and he's saying you ain't even close."

"Nonsense! Quality is in the eye of the beholder; *everyone* knows that!"

"Maybe. But there's more Oscars in his office than cars on the 405 freeway. That's why he insisted on processing your work: so he could monitor it. He knows his stuff, and he wants out."

"But we're already shooting! I've got the cast together, our leading lady is out of rehab..."

"Georgie, Georgie, baby, I know!"

"You could have said something earlier! Now we're stuck with a full staff and talent to pay!"

"Sorry, I didn't think to check that contract. I just never had to deal with the big-timers before. It's too late for regrets now. You'll have to let them go."

"But you don't *understand!* I can't *afford* to lay them off. We *have* to finish this project!"

"George, the backer baled! You got the Big Uh-Uh, nada, zip, Nowheresville. It's over."

George was trembling by then. "So what's a lousy million?" he whimpered. "Don't these people have any sense of Hollywood?"

"Um, this guy doesn't exactly see eye to eye with Hollywood. I'm sorry."

§

*"Tonight's real shocker is the unexpected cancellation of George's mega-epic 'The Zombies Who Ate Hollywood!', which shut down today when Marin County pulled their financial backing. The Producer/Director, George, that all too brief shining flash in the Hollywood sky, is reportedly tryin' to reach out to 'Marin County' for a deal. We haven't heard anythin' from the set, but rumors are the leadin' lady has gone into hidin'. What's sure is she and the leadin' man ah nowhere t' be seen..."*

George was no fool. He sent an intern—yes, he had interns all of a sudden—down to the studio to give them the bad news. That intern was never seen again. Morty, in the mean time, made a half-hearted effort to reason with 'Marin County', and was told abruptly never to darken that particular doorway again. He shrugged and gave up, regretting how a golden opportunity to get real financial backing for his thin cadre of losers had slipped through his fingers. Life went on.

*"Weah hearin' rumors of trouble on the set of that cancelled blockbuster 'The Zombies Who Ate Hollywood!' We haven't heard anythin' from the studio, but it seems they aren't happy with the delays in clearing their back lot. Meanwhile our sources tell us Producer/Director George, that falling star of the B epics, is tryin' t' get Marin County to reconsider..."*

Two weeks after the project was shut down, the set was still occupied by cast and crew. No one had seen any of the leading characters or the Producer/Director, but a horde of zombie extras were still on the set along with their decidedly rag-tag craft services crew. With the production cancelled, the studio wanted them cleared out so they could rent the back lot to another production, but they stayed there, day after day, ignoring phone calls and memos ordering them to vacate.

Meanwhile George was burning up the phone lines insisting, pleading, *begging* 'Marin County' to reconsider. The response was cold hostility at first. Soon they refused to return calls. Then they refused to accept calls. Letters came back unopened. George even took a Greyhound up there and tried to see them, but was turned away at the gate.

While this was going on, the studio management was finally fed up with the squatters on their priceless backlot. The head of the studio went storming down there in Righteous Wrath along with a half dozen studio security guards to tell them what for and hustle them off the property. Neither he nor the security guards were seen again, either.

In the meantime, the disappearances of homeless and vagrants continued. Soon street crime in Hollywood vanished, as did the nightlife. People whispered of some nameless terror roaming the streets, and barricaded their locked doors. Before long mailmen, delivery drivers, and even police patrols were disappearing...

§

The phone dragged Morty out of a sound sleep. He fumbled for it in the dark, only half awake. "Mnhgnmnbv?"

"Morty! We're in big trouble!"

"George?" Morty glanced at his bedside clock, and groaned. "D'you realize what time it is? *Why* are you calling me at two in the freakin' AM?"

"It's all gone t'hell, Marty..." There were screams and sirens in the background. "...No! Marty! Y'gotta help me...!" There was the sound of gunfire, and the phone went dead.

By time Morty got to his office, the city was in chaos. Traffic was at a standstill, the roads blocked with abandoned cars, and a building up the street was burning. The National Guard was deployed, and panicked refugees were fleeing every which way. "Jeez, this'd make great footage," he mumbled to himself.

"Morty!" It was George, looking more frazzled than usual. "I *told* you there'd be trouble! I *told* you we had to finish..."

He was interrupted by a rising chorus of screams and a fusillade of gunfire. The National Guardsmen were falling back before a solid wall of zombies stretching across the boulevard.

"What? Where'd they all come from? George?"

"Hey, it was Marin County! I told 'em we had some real backing for once. I was shooting for the big time."

"Georgie, dahling!" It was that hack Lou Ellen again, and she she was about to wet herself in excitement. "It's simply too, too fabulous! You really are the showman!"

"Lou Ellen, you need to get out of here, now!" George glanced nervously at the advancing mob. "Run, while you still can!"

"Ah just *love* it, Georgie, dahling!"

"No, really. Run!" The zombies were circling around them, pushing the retreating guardsmen back, moving in to surround them against the wall of an office building.

"Oh, really, Georgie! You think I *nevah* saw a Hollywood spectacle before? They'as so *many* extras! You must have an *unbelievable* advertisin' budget. Why, this'll make *all* the feature shows, and ah'll bet you'll make the evening news too!"

"You got that right," Morty whimpered.

"Lou Ellen..."

Too late: the wall of zombies closed around them, pinning them against the building. They pressed in from all sides...coming closer...and closer...until they became a solid mass of undead...who halted not more than twenty feet from them. There was an ugly silence broken by the sirens wailing in the distance and the muted rumble of thousands of zombies who stared at them with dead, hungry eyes.

"What are they waiting for?" George whimpered.

"Ah *love* their costuming! And they'ah makeup; Georgie, you really put on a show!"

Then there was a stir in their ranks, and a lone figure stepped to the front. He was tall and slender, impeccably dressed in an archaic tuxedo and flowing cape. His dark hair was combed back forming a pronounced widow's peak, and his chiseled face was ashen pale.

"Oh, Jesus!" Morty groaned.

George did a double-take. "You know this guy?"

"Yeah. He's the lawyer who handled the litigation after the original King Kong movie, back in the 30s."

"Huh? What?"

"Don't you remember? He filed a class action against the studio for all the collateral damage from the movie. It dragged on for years. He made them cough up for removing that huge ape carcass, repairs to the Empire State Building, compensation to the innocent bystanders hit by stray bullets from those Army biplanes, and even a bundle for the ape's family."

"No shit?"

"That's why the studio agreed to all those remakes and sequels in the years that followed: they needed the tax write-offs to pay litigation costs."

"Never heard of it."

"Why, Dahling, it was all ova the New York Post for *yeahs*," Lou Ellen gushed.

"So who reads the Post?"

The tall stranger halted in front of them and looked them over coldly. "My clients have retained me to address certain issues of non-performance," he said in a chilling whisper. "It seems you have reneged on an employment contract. They seek full redress, and are prepared to take action to enforce their claim."

"Ah *love* those fangs," Lou Ellen sighed. "What a *clevah* touch."

"W-we c-couldn't help it," George protested. "The backer cut our funding...w-we had to shut down..."

"Your financial arrangements are not my clients' concern. They have a contract, and they *insist* upon fulfillment."

"It's not our fault! This sort of thing happens all the time in Hollywood!"

Their lawyer gave him an icy look. "I think you will agree these circumstances aren't exactly *typical* of Hollywood. We *demand* you uphold the original contract, regardless of unforeseen circumstances on your part which have no bearing upon the performance as agreed by my clients. If you don't, we will have no choice but to seek recourse."

"Um...r-recourse?"

"Indeed. And we offer these tokens of our sincerity."

He turned and gestured to the wall of zombies behind him. Several of them shuffled forth and dropped the severed heads of the Studio Chairman and his chief of security at their feet. Their lifeless faces were frozen in uncomprehending horror.

"Shit, those are *real* zombies?" Lou Ellen's Brooklyn was as thick as it was shrill.

"I told you to run, Lou Ellen," George mumbled.

"And that's not all," the lawyer went on. "It seems employment opportunities for my clients are few and far between these days. In fact, you two are the only ones making zombie features. My clients *expect* long term job security as part of any settlement; specifically a steady stream of zombie productions in both theaters and television."

He was interrupted by a deep subliminal rumble of 'grrrrrr's from the surrounding crowd which sent chills down their spines. Their lawyer spread his arms in a gesture taking in his 'clients'. "So, you're going to finish this movie, unless you'd care to face a...um...labor action?" His smile was not pretty.

The shambling horde inched forward, 'grrrrrr'ing and drooling, staring at them with dead, hungry eyes. George stared at them in wide-eyed panic for a long moment, then turned to Morty. "Y-you were right about courtroom dramas all along, Morty," he said in a shaky whimper. "H-how much can you get me for 'The Zombies' Lawyer Who Ate Hollywood'?"

Morty eyed the slack-jawed, cadaverous horde around them nervously. "Um...how much do you want?"

*****

# "Divine Justice"

...and I'm all of a sudden standing on this white, foamy stuff...clouds? All around me is billowy white like a berserker detergent commercial, with a clear blue sky above like you'll never see without special filters. Whahoppin? Where's my Chinese carryout? Where did this ground fog come from? Where's the sidewalk? There's no buildings, no park bench, no restaurant, no J Avenue bus careening out of control...

Oops.

I look around frantically trying to find something familiar, but there is nothing but clouds and a clear blue sky bathed in radiant sunshine. "What th' hell? Oh!"

Not hell...

Then, right on cue, comes a roll of thunder, and the sky in front of me parts like a theatre curtain. Radiant golden light pours out with a chorus in the background doing that whole Hallelujah thing, and then the Big Dude himself appears. I hope t' tell you I'm shaken. I stand there mesmerized, staring up into a face the size of Texas while I take a hasty inventory of my life to see where I stand. As far as I can tell (seeing that I'm really distracted at the moment) He shouldn't have any grief with me. I lived a productive life. I earned an honest living and paid my bills and kept out of trouble. I wasn't into any kind of kinky sex. And I helped that little old lady across the street last month. Unless he's gonna get picky about those shoplifted candy bars, I should be okay.

He stares down at me for a long moment, and I start wondering where I'd seen that face before. There's something naggingly familiar about Him. I can't put my finger on it, but it's definitely there. He looks like...nah, not him; or like...no, not that either; He looks like...well...He looks like an *editor*. That...isn't comforting...

"YOU HAVE COME TO JUDGEMENT. WOEFUL IS YOUR LIFE, AND NOW YOUR SOUL MUST BE WEIGHED," God says.

"Huh? What'ja mean my soul must be weighed? What'd I do?"

"YOUR FAILINGS ARE GRIEVOUS AND MANY," God says.

"What?  No one's perfect.  I've been a decent sort."

"I SHALL BE THE JUDGE OF THAT," God says.

"Hay, look, man, this isn't about that drug thing?" I says.  "'cause that was the 60s, you know?" I says.  "That was Nam and Watergate, and up there in the Village was a whole different scene," I says.

"SHUT UP," God says.

" " I says.

"YOUR PETTY INDISCRETIONS DO NOT MATTER.  YOUR SOUL IS WEIGHED DOWN BY A LIFETIME OF DEBASED AND DEGRADING TOIL BY WHICH YOU EARNED AN UNJUST LIVING."

"My writing?"

"WELL?"

"What?  So I'm self-published?  So I didn't get a Pulitzer?  Is it my fault the Eastern Establishment is a bunch of blind, stupid pigs?  My stuff sells to the webzines and at the cons just fine, thank you very much, so what's your problem?"

"YOUR LIFE'S WORKS ARE AN EXCRETION UPON THE FACE OF THE UNIVERSE!"

"*Everyone's* a critic!  *Jee-zus* H Christ!"

"LET'S KEEP FAMILY OUT OF THIS."  My ass is zapped by a lightning bolt.

"OWWWWW!  Sorry..."

"SO HOW DO YOU EXPLAIN THIS?" He demands as words appear in the air between us, "D'YOU CALL *THIS* WRITING?"

*It was a dark and stormy night when*
*the stranger rode into town.*

"Aw, now wait just a *minute!*" I pout.  "It can be a dark and stormy night, just the same as any other kind of night, can't it?  And if the stranger *didn't* ride into town, there wouldn't be much of a story, would there?"

A moments pause.  "HMMM, I SUPPOSE YOU HAVE ME ON THAT."

"Yeah, right.  So what's your problem?"

172

# IT'S SCHLOCK!!!!

"...uh...gee, that's...that's really neat...with the thunder and all... Love the effect."  Gosh, I didn't know you could wet yourself in Heaven.

"ASIDE FROM WHICH, IT'S PLAGIARISM.  HAVE YOU NO SHAME?"

"Hey, it's public domain, and there aren't any original plots any more.  Besides, I can write what I damn well please...OWWW!!! Dammit!" Another lightning bolt.

"LANGUAGE."  He waves a massive finger at me.

I'm beginning to see this guy has a real weed up his arse about literature.  "I get it.  You're one of those anti-science fiction types, ain't ya?   You're afraid of new ideas; afraid people will start thinking on their own.  You're no better than the Republicans..."

WHAM!   That one throws me twenty feet and leaves me sprawled on my face with the seat of my 501s smoldering. "*DON'T* TRY THAT FALSE EQUIVALENCY WITH *ME!*"

"You probably watch Fox, don'tja?" I mutter sullenly.

"I DO *NOT!*  AND YOUR WRITING HARDLY REQUIRES THINKING.  SEE FOR YOURSELF."  More words in the air:

> *He looked upon the lean, cat-like form of the Yeoman, and could tell from her fulsome bodice that she was ripe for the Y-ovyalnn, the Perpetual Mating.  The smoldering gleam in her eyes and her deep, subaudible growl said she'd chosen him to be her next conquest.  The way her furry tail whipped and curled warned him that she was a skilled priestess in the Cult of Eros...*

"Hey, I love that part!  She's one of my favorite characters, and every story needs a love interest.  What's wrong with that?  You're not into some kind of alien prejudice, are you?"

"IT IS AN INSULT TO GOOD TASTE, TO SAY NOTHING OF BORING. WHY CAN'T YOU WRITE QUALITY FICTION LIKE ROBERT L FORWARD DID?"

"I knew Bob Forward, heck of a nice guy. I kept telling him he should write a book called 'Astrophysics For Dummies'...OWW!!! Enough with the lightning bolts, already!"

"AND YOUR SYNTAX IS TERRIBLE, NOT TO MENTION YOUR PUNCTUATION GIVES ME A HEADACHE."

"Hey, *you* invented commas. Don't blame *me* for that!"

"YOUR CHARACTERS ARE SHALLOW AND TWO-DIMENSIONAL, YOUR ACTION SEQUENCES ARE CLUNKY, AND YOUR INFO-DUMPS GIVE ME INDIGESTION."

"It's not *my* fault the New York market wouldn't touch me! If you're so all wise and all benevolent, why couldn't you arrange an Agent for me? How am I supposed to write the Great American Novel without the help of an editor?"

"I GAVE MORTAL MAN THE GIFT OF LANGUAGE THAT HE MIGHT EXHALT IN REASON AND WISDOM, BUT YOU DENIGRATED IT WITH YOUR VAPID, INTELLECTUALLY ILLITERATE SENSATIONALISM."

"Well, yeah, maybe. But it's great fun! And how many Sci Fi readers are really into astrophysics, anyway? Really? Or bioengineering? Or stellar mechanics? Huh? They just want a slam-bang good story! A guy's gotta go where the market is."

"I GAVE MORTAL MAN THE GIFT OF WRITING, AND YOU PERVERTED IT WITH YOUR TRASHY HACKMEISTERING!"

"But I never wrote campaign ads..."

"I GAVE MORTAL MAN THESE GIFTS, AND YOU USED THEM TO CREATE MINDLESS AMUSEMENT! FOR YOU THERE CAN BE ONLY ONE JUSTICE!"

"Hey, at least I was never on TV." Even as I whine that, I know it isn't helping my case, not one little bit...

"AS YE HAVE SOWN, SO SHALL YE REAP!"

And God waves His hand...

And I cringe...

§

*...and I'm sitting in a great elevated Command Chair! A broad, sweeping Command Deck spreads around me, with banks of control stations arrayed before the vast viewscreen, and multiple displays overhead lit up to show the status of the ship! Strong, proud Stellar Marines sitting at those stations, tall, buff, rock solid, with clear eyes and firm jaws like you only see in recruiting posters, glance at me and nod, affirming me as one of them!*

*Then I realize where I am: on the bridge of the Grand Battleship 'Majestic'! The Grand Galactic Imperial Stellar Fleet is all around us on the viewscreens! Stars are whipping past the viewports, Arciline purple and Vermentic orange and Diphlunium blue, faster and faster as our mighty Gernsbach engines thunder and rave against the bounds of reality! This is the opening scene of my first novel, 'The War Gods Of Altair Six!'*

*There's a subaudible growl behind me! I turn, and there she is: tall, lean, lathe, steaming golden eyes, unbearably hot; priestess of the Cult of Eros! My personal Yeoman! The look in her eyes and her subtile nod toward my ready room leaves no doubt as to her intentions!*

*I don't get it! If I'm to be eternally damned, then why send me here?! I've written dozens of stories in this series, when I'm not daydreaming about swashbuckling adventure with my heroic band of space mercenaries! This is hardly my idea of hell! Then it all adds up: that guy must be one of those stick-in-the-mud intellectuals, that whole All Wise, All Knowing thing: figures! He probably masturbates while reading Proust! To Him, this is eternal damnation!*

*I take another bold look at the Yeoman, and wonder how she ever managed to get into that tiny bodice! Her eyes smolder as she toys with the bottle of Passionflower Nectar suspended from her collar! As I recall, we have six days until we reach enemy space! Yeah, I'll manage!*

*I just hope I can find time to catch up on my writing!*

\*\*\*\*\*

# Titles from The Written Wyrd
## 2021-22

**The Diplomacy Trilogy** - Science fiction humor.
First contact from the aliens' perspective in a trio of lurid tell-all memoirs written by a team of alien diplomats sent to earth to open an embassy.

**The MacKenna Trilogy** - Science fiction military drama.
He was earth's greatest soldier; they needed his skills once more, but they didn't realize how wrong bringing him back from the dead was.

**Nature's Way** - Environmental disaster / apocalyptic horror.
This is the last day of our last stand against Nature out for revenge!

**Trial** - Science fiction political thriller.
The aliens demand justice for their murdered ambassador while right wing extremists plot revolution; which is the greater threat?

**Overland** - Period science fiction drama / romance.
He was trapped between a beautiful genetically enhanced revolutionary from the distant future and the inhuman monster sent to destroy her.  Can he survive caught up in their titanic battle?

**Playing God** - Apocalyptic horror.
Brenda discovers she is the Dream Girl of a mad scientist capable of altering the past.  Can she find a way to undo the disaster he wrought and prevent a nuclear holocaust?

**The Big Snow** - Environmental disaster / adventure.
A passenger train is wrecked at the top of Donner Pass in the worst storms in recorded history.  Can the railroaders get the passengers to safety?

(continued)

## Young Adult Demi-Novels:

**Diplomacy's Children** - YA humor / adventure.
A young alien space fleet recruit faces his greatest challenge in a self-centered, foul-tempered human youngling he is ordered to keep in check.

**Star Flight** - YA adventure.
She was an outcast, cursed with supernatural powers. She was offered a reprieve, a chance to start over, but could she survive the challenge?

## Short Story Anthologies:

**Deus Ex Machina** - Humorous fantasy short story collection.
From bungling wizards to moronic barbarians to redneck elves, here are the old tales of epic adventure as we would love to see them told - just once.

**Ghoulish Good Fun** - Macabre short story collection.
Reality is a cruel practical joke. Laugh along with it if you dare!

\*\*\*\*\*

Available in print and Kindle from Amazon.
Visit our web site for details.

**http://www.the-written-wyrd.org/shopping.shtml**

## A Brief Note From The Author

Thank you for reading this collection of my more off-the-wall humor. It is rare that an author gets to indulge in sheer cynical whimsey like this, and I hope it was a good read for you. I would love to hear from you, my readers, to let me know how I am doing as an author. Every bit of input helps me to make my next effort a better product for your enjoyment.

All my best,

Bob Boyd

You can learn more about me, and keep up to date on my efforts through our Blog:

### Facebook.com/The Written Wyrd

\*\*\*\*\*

www.ingramcontent.com/pod-product-compliance
Lightning Source LLC
Chambersburg PA
CBHW072124170626
46813CB00004B/1689